What the critics are saying…

"Christmas in Virginia is stellar contemporary romance that will leave readers looking for Mlyn Hurn's other titles." It "provides romance, hot sex scenes, a scheming ex-husband and family humor making…" this "…a book that I can't recommend highly enough." ~ *CIV Review Fallen Angel*

"*Christmas in Virginia* is a heartwarming story of two people finding love again. …Displays all the emotions that Jack and Laena go through to find love again, from intrusive relatives and exes that will not leave them alone, to the doubt that plagues their minds. …A wonderful story that I could not put down." ~ *CIV Review_Road to Romance*

Mlyn Hurn

Christmas in Virginia

ELLORA'S CAVE
ROMANTICA PUBLISHING

An Ellora's Cave Romantica Publication

www.ellorascave.com

Christmas in Virginia

ISBN # 1419952137
ALL RIGHTS RESERVED.
Christmas in Virginia Copyright© 2004 Mlyn Hurn
Edited by: Linda Carroll-Bradd
Cover art by: Syneca

Electronic book Publication: December, 2004
Trade paperback Publication: June, 2005

Excerpt from *Cattleman* Copyright © Mlyn Hurn, 2004

Warning:

The following material contains graphic sexual content meant for mature readers. *Christmas in Virginia* has been rated *S-ensuous* by a minimum of three independent reviewers.

Ellora's Cave Publishing offers three levels of Romantica™ reading entertainment: S (S-ensuous), E (E-rotic), and X (X-treme).

S-ensuous love scenes are explicit and leave nothing to the imagination.

E-rotic love scenes are explicit, leave nothing to the imagination, and are high in volume per the overall word count. In addition, some E-rated titles might contain fantasy material that some readers find objectionable, such as bondage, submission, same sex encounters, forced seductions, etc. E-rated titles are the most graphic titles we carry; it is common, for instance, for an author to use words such as "fucking", "cock", "pussy", etc., within their work of literature.

X-treme titles differ from E-rated titles only in plot premise and storyline execution. Unlike E-rated titles, stories designated with the letter X tend to contain controversial subject matter not for the faint of heart.

Also by Mlyn Hurn:

Christmas in Virginia

Chapter One

Jack Spencer parked his car at the lower end of his sister Cindy's drive. He knew he was the last to arrive, but at the last minute, he hadn't been able to leave the office as originally planned. The rest of the family had probably arrived several hours earlier, as he had wanted to do. He'd known his mother was arriving a day earlier than everyone else, and he'd hoped to spend some time with her privately.

Jack climbed out of his luxury sedan and started up the drive, carrying his overnight bag. Immediately he noticed the Christmas decorations along both sides of the long path. They seemed at odds with the unusually warm weather. Across the lawn were several wired shapes, which he recognized as lighted animal shapes. Frowning, he remembered the last time he'd seen those had been in his mother's lawn. What were they doing here?

With a shrug and a small smile, he recognized the cars as he passed them. The one he parked directly behind was a dirty full-sized truck, and he knew it belonged to his next younger brother, Patrick. He farmed the land of their father, grandfather and great-grandfather. He noticed it was a newer version of truck than last time he'd seen him. This one had the longer cab. Pat had probably gotten it because his two sons were now teens, and probably had legs as long as Pat's. He considered it a miracle that Jean,

Pat's wife of almost twenty years, was still with him. She had the patience of Job to put up with Pat and two sons.

Parked on the far side of the truck was a jaunty secondhand sports car. He had purchased the car for his twin sons, David and Daniel, two years ago when they headed off to college. He was glad the boys were here already because it would be nice to spend some extra time with them if he could. The last eight years had been hard on them all. His wife, Celia, had died two years before the first election, when the boys were just nine. Both his and Celia's mothers had been godsends. He never would have made it without them.

Sometimes he wondered if he shouldn't have quit after the successful campaign for re-election. Since his whole family was used to the shift in their lives, and with his sons' approval, he'd chosen to continue serving. The honest truth was that he'd enjoyed every tense, important and often frustrating moment of the Harding Administration.

Jack stopped abruptly as a flash of bright red nearer the house caught his eye. He expected the closest car to the house to be his mother's, but he didn't recognize it. No way could a car like this belong to his mother. Ruth drove a very sensible, four-door brown sedan. This was a cherry red convertible. Even though the weather was unseasonably warm, he was surprised to see the top down. He noticed the white leather interior and shook his head. He couldn't imagine who in hell would drive a car like that!

Just then, a ball flew out from behind the house. A little girl, about eight years old or so followed it. As she neared, he recognized Kristi, his sister Janet's youngest.

He wondered where her twin, Karen, was since they were seldom parted.

She saw him and stopped chasing the ball. Her voice was extremely loud as she practically screamed to get everyone's attention, "Uncle Jack is here."

In just a few seconds, he was besieged by a fair number of teenagers, and little Kristi who demanded to be picked up.

David picked up the petite little girl, and then put her on his shoulders. She squealed her delight, her fingers clutching his hair.

Daniel reached out and took his father's bag. Both boys greeted their dad with a smile.

Jack felt a momentary pang, remembering the days when they would run up to hug him. But they were both tall, at least six feet, and well-built young men. They had their mother's dark hair and eyes. Before he could say anything, he heard his mother calling out for everyone to come to the backyard because the food was ready. *Today doesn't seem like Christmas*, Jack thought sadly. The temperature was unseasonably warm enough for everyone to be running around outdoors in shorts, and they were cooking on the grill.

Jack laughed when he saw his mother dressed in a white apron, sporting a huge red lobster on it and a tall, white chef's hat. She had a long fork in her hand and was obviously in charge of the grill. He saw his two sisters, Janet and Cindy, seated at one of the long picnic tables. His three sisters-in-law joined them—Jean, Felicia and Sally. They all waved, but didn't stop their engrossing conversation.

He walked over to his mother and kissed her cheek lightly. "It's good to see you, Mother," he told her softly.

Ruth paused and saw the tinge of sadness in his eyes. He was a hard man to the world, but he would always be her firstborn, her baby. He was the image of his father John. He had his father's blond hair, now graying a bit. His eyes were just as clear and blue as her husband's had been. He was about six foot tall, and while his suits always concealed his body, she knew he had a hard, muscular physique from long workouts to relieve the stress of his job.

He had been the youngest man ever to hold his position in the government. And his good friend Thomas Harding had been a young president. They had learned together, making mistakes along the way. She was glad he would be out of the rat race soon. He had received quite a few offers to join different prestigious law firms, but he had not yet committed himself. No doubt, he would be spending the next days and weeks deciding where his future lay. She tried not to show how much she wished he would settle here, in the area. He had missed out on so much of his family, and the changes they had gone through. His sons would definitely benefit from having their father closer at hand.

"You look tired, John," she told him softly, smiling at him.

Jack grimaced. His mother was the only one to ever call him by his given name. Since grade school, all of his friends had called him "Spence" or like family, they called him "Jack". Even in the White House, he had been known as Spence. He nodded as he replied. "Not much longer, Mom, since the new guy takes over January twentieth. I'll come home and sleep in my old bed. Then it will be just you and me to rattle around in that big, old house together."

He kissed her cheek, turning away as his brothers called out his name. As he turned, he thought a brief look of confusion appeared on his mother's face as a flush stained her barely wrinkled cheeks. But pushing away the concern, he figured it was just his own tiredness making him see things.

Jack walked to where his brothers were trying to put up a net of some kind. He assumed they were running out of ideas to occupy all the kids. His brothers greeted him jokingly, calling him the "old man" and how it took him long enough to get there. Jack just stood for a few moments, taking in the wonderful feeling of being amongst family once again.

At one of the nets stood his oldest brother Patrick and Phil, who squatted down, retying the ropes to the stakes. Phillip was fourth oldest at forty-three years, and a very successful lawyer with a large and prestigious firm just outside of Washington, near Arlington. Their daughter Melissa, at only fifteen years of age, was just as beautiful as her mother, Felicia. As a senior partner of the firm, Felicia's father had approached him to join as a full senior partner without any buy-in. Jack was having misgivings since his brother Phillip was a partner, and had been with the firm since he graduated from law school. He didn't want to cause problems by joining.

The far end of the net had his youngest brother Michael occupied. *Hard to believe Michael had turned forty.* Jack looked around for Michael's wife, Sally. Their three children—Mandy, sixteen, and twin boys, Tracy and Terry, just turned fourteen in November—kept her running sometimes. Before he found Sally, he heard his baby sister, Janet, younger than him by ten years, yelling at her husband, Tom Tiner.

"Tom! The girls are trying to steal your ball again!"

Jack looked to where Tom stood beside Michael, and Chris and John, who were Patrick's two teenaged sons.

Tom pointed towards his twin girls, who were giggling as they struggled over the same ball. "Chris, John! Retrieve the ball, please."

Jack laughed as the teen boys loped good-naturedly after the girls. *God! It felt good to be home.*

"Jack! Have mercy, man! I thought you'd come dressed to play!"

He grinned at Cindy's husband Hank, who worked as vice president of the local bank. "I'll change later. It was cooler in DC."

"You can be the judge then. We should be eating pretty soon anyway." He walked away to add his opinion to Michael's efforts with the ropes.

Jack slowly let his gaze wander across the large, open yard, taking in the family gathered there. He grimaced as he realized how many teenagers were going to be in the house at one time. Slowly, thinking how quickly the last ten years had passed, he smiled. Caught up first with his wife Celia's illness, and then her death, followed by the frenetic pace of the campaign, and then by serving as Chief of Staff for two terms had been arduous on the easiest of days. And now, only twenty-eight more days remained before they all left the White House, after nearly eight years, for the last time.

He shook his head sadly, amazed at how quickly time had gone by. He didn't regret the last eight years, but he knew the time away had taken a toll on his family, especially his boys, and Ruth. His mother was sixty-nine now, and while she was still pretty active, he worried about her. She was alone in the huge house where she'd raised her six children, and even though Patrick's house on the farmland was only about a mile away, they all still worried.

He turned to ask Pat about the farm, when he heard someone calling for some help. Jack noticed that all of his brothers and brothers-in-law had looked towards the woman asking for assistance. Without giving it much thought, he glanced around to see what was garnering such rapt attention.

Chapter Two

A woman stood on the back steps, just outside the kitchen door. She carried a heavily laden tray and tried to hold onto several sacks of buns. Jack noticed several things all at once. First, she barely got the words out of her mouth before she was deluged with offers of help from his sons and Pat's two boys. Laughing, she let the four young men take different things from her.

Jack then noticed how beautiful she was. She had long, sun-streaked blonde hair and was obviously tan. She was probably about five and a half feet tall. What was quite remarkable was her stunning figure, and it was shown off to advantage in jean shorts and white cotton shirt, which was tied high on her midriff, just below her full and obviously unbound breasts.

Jack turned to ask one of his brothers who the woman was, but the words died on his lips as he saw the stunned looks on their faces. Jack shifted around and looked at the table where the women were seated. He noticed that they were all hunched forward and whispering furiously. Jack didn't know the stranger, but it was obvious she was a disruptive force in the house. Deciding to discover her identity, he started to call out to his nearest brother. Abruptly he stopped when he heard his mother talking.

"Laena, dear, come over here. I want you to meet my oldest boy, John."

Jack took a step forward, to go back over to his mother. He thought he heard one of his brothers mutter something that sounded like "good luck" before he was too far away. He'd barely come to his mother's side when she reached out to him with her hand. He took it and let her pull him close. Half-listening to his mother, he looked the woman over in detail. He scoffed at himself as he realized that he had already spent a fair amount of time assessing the woman's attractions.

Her eyes were a dark blue, almost like the bluish-purple of pansies. He could see she wore no makeup, but her lashes were a dark blondish-brown and matched her brows. She was smiling at his mother, and he could see her lips were full and curved, revealing her white, straight teeth. He looked down quickly and took in the firm, full breasts that were pressed against the white cotton shirt. The shorts were a little loose, and fell to just below her waist, revealing a perfect belly button. He started to look back up when he noticed the small gold ring that pierced her skin.

When he returned to her face, Jack was chagrined to discover the woman was watching him stare at her body. He couldn't help the bright flush that stained his cheeks. He felt like a gauche schoolboy who had just gotten caught staring at a stolen centerfold picture. The analogy was apt, he told himself silently. She had the kind of body one always saw in a flashy magazine, the kind that came with a foldout.

Laena Hunt held out her hand towards the man she had seen countless times on the news, and in many pictures around Ruth's house. From infant, to toddler, first-grader, teenager and finally college graduate. She felt she knew him from all the stories Ruth had shared with her over the last few months. It took a moment before Jack took her hand. His grip was firm, what you would expect from a politician, she told herself with a small smile. She looked into his face, but could read nothing. Then she heard him repeat her name. She wanted to deny the shiver that chased up her arm and through her spine at the touch of his hand to hers. She turned as she realized Ruth was speaking to her.

"Laena, dear, you get something to eat first and go sit down. You have done all the work this afternoon. John, dear, you sit with Laena and make her feel at home. I'll join you both in a few minutes."

Laena accepted a hot dog and went over to get a bun. She put a few other things on her plate, aware that Jack Spencer was following right behind her. She went to the farthest picnic table, which she had been getting used to sharing with the children. They all seemed to like her. She was intensely aware of the negative looks she always received from Ruth's daughters and daughters-in-law. A moment later, Jack took the seat opposite her. She told him quickly, "You should change your clothes, Mr. Spencer. The wood on these benches is a little rough and might ruin that nice suit."

Jack looked up and met Laena's gaze, seeing the sincerity on her face. "It will be fine for the short time I'll be out here. I'll change after we all eat."

He watched her take a bite of her hot dog, almost staring as her white teeth bit through the hot dog and bun. He was jolted to his core as he felt a searing bolt of arousal shoot through him. Immediately he wondered how those pretty white teeth might feel nipping at his flesh. Damn! He hadn't felt this kind of attraction to a woman since his wife had died. Basically, he'd been too damned busy the last eight years. Perhaps, feeling a moment of humor come over him, he should be grateful she wasn't watching her carb-intake and eating the hot dog without the bun. He opened his mouth to question just who exactly she was, but suddenly he was distracted as both his sons joined the table, sitting on either side of Laena.

Both boys started talking at the same time, and Jack watched how she juggled the two young men. She talked to them both equally, and was very careful he noticed, not to be too friendly with either one. He realized with a start of surprise that his sons were young men. And obviously, they were now attracted to women, not just young girls their own age. Jack took a deep breath, preparing to try and speak to Laena again. Before he could say a word, Pat's two sons were jostling him, sitting on either side. Chris and John were obviously just as smitten with the beauty seated opposite him as his own two sons were.

Over the next few minutes, the four younger men competed actively for Laena's attention, barely giving her a chance to eat. Jack got the distinct impression this was not the first time this scenario had been enacted, either. Before he could think of a way to interrupt the youthful conversation, his mother arrived.

Ruth told all four boys to move on without the slightest bit of compunction, she needed to talk with Laena, and it was ages since she'd had lunch with her oldest son.

The four boys obeyed their grandmother, even if reluctantly.

Ruth sat next to Laena, which surprised Jack. He thought she would sit next to him. He was going to have to get to the bottom of this mystery. Just who was this young woman, and what part was she playing, if any, in his mother's life?

Ruth took a bite of the potato salad and complimented Laena on it. She looked at Jack and commented casually on what a good cook Laena was.

Jack caught the surprised look the younger woman gave the older one, and saw the blush steal up over her tanned cheeks. He nodded and agreed that it was quite tasty. He looked at Laena and asked, "What do you do for a living, Ms. Hunt?"

Before Laena could reply, his mother answered, "Laena isn't working right now, John. She is staying with me, at the house."

Jack was aware of his mother staring, and from the look on her face, he could tell that her mind was actively working on something.

A few moments later, his mother questioned him. "What did you think of my new car, John?"

Jack looked from Laena to his mother, hoping for a moment his confusion wasn't grossly obvious on his face. "New car?" he asked tersely. It appeared his mother had experienced a number of new things since this young woman entered his family's lives. "When did you buy a new car?" Taking a deep breath, he silently reminded himself to stay calm. After all, he was supposed to be relaxing and taking it easy from the rigors of his job. But he also knew that his mother had bought only two cars since his father's death, and he had been with her both times.

Ruth grinned and glanced at Laena before she turned back to her son. "I thought for sure you would have seen it, dear. The red convertible next to the house."

Jack choked on the bite he had just taken. He coughed, and his mother hopped up and hurried around to pound on his back. He heard through the commotion that Laena told everyone to leave him alone because he was still getting air in. If he started to truly choke, she would perform the Heimlich on him. She handed him some water and told him to sip it slowly. He did and stopped coughing a moment later. He had tears in his eyes as he met her steady gaze. She was the only one who had remained calm, other than his brother, Michael, the doctor in the family.

As his mother resumed her seat next to Laena, both his sisters sat on either side of him.

Janet spoke first. "Are you all right, Jack? What upset you?"

Jack turned to look at his youngest sister. He recognized the look on her face and knew that she was fishing to see if he was as worried about what had the two of them concerned. He didn't have to guess the worry was the beautiful woman seated across from him. He smiled at Janet. "I had just taken a bite and was a little surprised to discover Mother has a new car."

Before Janet or Cindy could say anything, Ruth spoke, "I quite adore my new little car. I don't drive it much. Laena is usually the one doing the driving and running my errands for me. And I must say that all of the boys have certainly enjoyed taking rides with her in the car."

Laena flushed at Ruth's words. She had caught the looks Jack had given her when the boys were at the table. She figured he was seeing her as a femme fatale, and a stealer of young men's innocence. Those boys were far from innocent. From some of the things they had told her jokingly so far, she had no doubt the twins had enjoyed a broad high school and then college experience.

Laena grabbed her plate and stood. "I'll start cleaning up. The rest of you enjoy your visit." She darted across the lawn and was inside in just a few seconds.

Jack was aware his sisters had already started talking to their mother, and rather heatedly. He quickly learned Laena had come to live with their mother a few months ago. Ruth experienced a few dizzy spells, and the doctor suggested several different options. She could sell the house and move in with one of the children. The next option was for Ruth to move into a retirement community, or lastly, get a live-in companion. Obviously, she had taken the latter course. And it was clear the two sisters thought the young woman was going to take advantage of their mother.

Jack stood abruptly. "I hope you don't mind if I go in and change out of this suit, Cindy."

Cindy shook her head and told him he had the room at the front of the house.

Jack nodded and reclaimed his bag. He made his way upstairs and found the room his sister always saved for him. The room was unusually large, and it connected to another bedroom. Cindy never put anyone else in the other room, knowing that Jack needed as much privacy and quiet as possible. When he managed to get some free time away from the political hubbub, he often used the other bedroom as a mini-office, setting up his computer and fax. During those times, his rooms were off-limits to everyone.

He unpacked quickly and was glad he had thrown in a pair of jean shorts. A few minutes later, he made his way down the backstairs. He walked into the kitchen, stopping as he saw Laena standing at the sink, up to her elbows in soap bubbles.

As silent as a panther, he walked into the kitchen, glancing out the window at the backyard. He saw his sisters and three sisters-in-law still sitting and talking. His mother was playing with the younger children, and his brothers were back to fiddling with the net. He moved over until he was just a foot or so behind her before he spoke. "Who made you the kitchen maid?"

Laena jumped, spinning in surprise. She slipped on the splashed water, and Jack reached out to grab her arms and steady her. Startled, she glanced up and met his gaze. She wanted to deny the electricity her body was feeling at his touch. Her brain was telling her body these feelings were ridiculous. She raised her hands and pressed against Jack's broad chest. She planned on pushing him away, but she felt the muscles ripple beneath the soft T-shirt he wore. Her soapy, wet hands lingered.

Big mistake—no, huge mistake—she realized as her body absorbed the warmth coming from his body. More than just comfy-cozy heat surrounded her. This was hot, uncomfortable and had her feeling certain things in places she'd hoped were dead, at least for a while longer. The last thing she needed... No! She pushed the unfinished thought out of her head. This man was nothing more than the son of the woman that she was caring for at the moment. He'd be gone soon, surely!

Jack argued with himself to let her go, but his hands wouldn't release the grip he had on her. If anything, he moved a little closer as he met her eyes. The searing heat he felt when he touched her was unnerving. He had been living a basically celibate life for ten years. And now, he was getting hard at the sight of her curvy, womanly body.

He argued with his logical, rational side. But his body was winning, and his arms pulled her closer. And then, she raised her hands to his chest. His heart started racing at the feel of her wet hands pressing on his chest. He pulled her more firmly, overcoming her strength pushing against him. He wanted to kiss her. *Hell*, Jack acknowledged reluctantly to himself, *he wanted to press her down on his sister's kitchen table and fuck her*. His head bent towards her. He would have kissed her, if the screen door behind them hadn't slammed shut.

Laena moved away from Jack at the same instant he released her. She spun back to the sink, and Jack greeted his youngest niece.

Kristi instantly started chattering away, completely unaware of the tensions or of the confrontation she had interrupted.

Jack finally figured out why the little girl had come into the house and helped her fill a small saucer with milk for the new kittens living in the garage. He turned after holding open the door and looked at Laena's stiff back. Quietly, he moved across the large kitchen and rested his back against the counter beside her, arms folded across his chest. He watched the play of emotions across her face, even though she didn't say a word. He finally asked her softly, "Who are you and why are you living with my mother?"

Laena started in surprise. She had not been expecting *him* to question her on this subject. Not that she was getting used to the sly innuendoes and half-asked questions from the others. But after the tension-filled seconds a short time earlier, she had thought he would have something else on his mind. After all, it remained first and foremost in her thoughts. And of course, it was absolutely the only thing her body was focused on. Every part of her sensed his nearness, and yearned to turn towards him.

She took a deep breath of relief. Her subconscious recognized it wasn't real, but thinking that seemed to help. She lifted one hand, pushing her hair back off her face, before she continued to wash the dishes. She could shrug his question off, but she doubted he would accept that.

Jack watched the simple movement and his gaze moved down to her full breasts. From this angle and proximity, he could see the deep cleavage between her breasts. His eyes fell just another few inches and he saw her nipples now poked little tents into her white cotton shirt. He couldn't stop the small smile from curving his lips. He was glad to see she was just as aroused as he had been. Though a fair amount of time had passed, he admitted that he was probably rusty in knowing whether a woman was attracted to him or not. His gaze returned to her face as she answered him.

"I like Ruth. She needed someone to stay with her, and I needed somewhere to live for a bit. Then we luckily discovered that we had a lot of interests to share." She paused. "And you all have quite a gem in Ruth, though I think some of you have forgotten it." She pulled the plug, letting the water drain. She picked up the hand spray and turned on the hot water to rinse the dishes one more time.

Jack watched as she slowly and carefully rinsed the dishes. "I'd *recommend* you start wearing a bra. We've got too many teenaged boys here with raging hormones for you to be shaking your tits at them all day."

Laena gasped in surprise at his words. The nozzle slipped from her hand, spraying water madly for the few seconds it took Jack to reach over and turn off the water. His words had caught her totally by surprise. She had given no thought to what she wore lately. Her appearance had sunk to the bottom of her priority list, and she usually just pulled on old clothes. If she could find her makeup, it was probably dried and beyond use. To be honest, her mind was rarely on what was happening around her. She had taken the boys' attention as just being friendly. Mostly she brushed off their antics as teen hormones.

She turned to look at Jack. It took a moment to realize that *he* was looking at her chest. She glanced down and gasped in surprise. Obviously, her chest had taken the brunt of the water spray. Her shirt was damp and plastered to her breasts. Coming on top of his suggestion a few moments earlier, it was too much. If the spraying had lasted longer, she would now look naked. She should be grateful for small graces.

She glanced up, wanting to say something really biting and scathing. Her half-formed words died though as she saw the look of blatant lust on his face as he looked at her body. Her nipples were tight and distended, making obvious tents in her shirt. Her breasts looked even bigger than her usual D cup. She gasped and spun away from him in disgust at herself. Before Jack could come up with something to say, she ran up the back staircase to her room.

Chapter Three

Jack turned to follow, when the door opened and closed, admitting his brother Pat. He was grinning as he came in, and Jack wondered how much he had heard outside the screen door.

Pat went to the refrigerator and pulled out more ice from the top freezer. He turned and was still grinning.

Jack glared. "What are you grinning about?"

"Well, funny thing actually. I was helping little Kristi give some milk to the kittens, and she was telling me the strangest story. Of course, I didn't believe her. And then she said her 'Uncle Jack had handprints on his shirt'."

As Pat paused, Jack looked down at his shirt. He saw that Laena's hands had indeed left two obvious hand marks on his shirt, just over his pectoral muscles. He saw that his nipples were poking against his shirt. He looked back up angrily and found Pat was still grinning.

Pat moved to the door. "I would change shirts, though, big brother." Pat grinned, glancing over his shoulder. "Unless you want Cindy and Janet to tear you apart." The door slammed shut behind him.

Jack sprinted up the back stairs to his room. He didn't think about there being one extra person than usual in the house until he was passing the small bedroom next to his. The door hadn't closed completely and even though his logic, and just about everything else except his body, told him to walk on, he didn't. He gave a gentle push to the door and it swung open silently. He stepped into the room and saw a wet white shirt tossed onto the twin-size bed. He heard sounds coming from the bathroom that connected the two bedrooms. He quickly backed out and went around to his room. He tossed off his own shirt and, as nonchalantly as he could, pushed open the bathroom door.

Laena froze in surprise as she saw Jack reflected in the mirror. She had never considered that he would be in the next bedroom. And then, she remembered where they were. She dropped her arms, covering her half-clad breasts. She had put on a bra, but it was more revealing than anything else, leaving almost the entire top half of her breasts exposed and just barely covering her nipples.

The reflection showed Jack as he leaned against the doorframe, not even bothering to look away. "That might fit the category of a bra, but it's not really much of an improvement."

Laena felt the fiery flush of embarrassment that moved up her chest and finally heated her cheeks. Her breath dragged harshly and unevenly in and out of her lungs. Telling herself that she hated feeling this way, still hesitating to call it an attraction, she slowly set down the brush. Quickly she moved her hand back to its protective stance. "I'm sorry if my clothes don't meet your standards, but I didn't pack to impress for this holiday. I'll run home and get some other clothes after I get dressed."

Jack shifted his stance, taking a half step forward and raising his hands to either side of the doorframe. His move only made his appearance more intently masculine to Laena, and more arousing. He smiled as he spoke, "Throw a shirt on and I'll drive you."

"That won't be necessary, I can drive myself." She turned her back and walked into her bedroom. She found a navy blue T-shirt and pulled it on over her head. She turned and found that Jack had followed her into her bedroom. She could feel her cheeks flushing even brighter.

"You've got five cars blocking you in, and mine's the last. It only makes sense for me to drive you over there," Jack told her.

Even though he didn't smile, she sensed that he was pleased with the information he had just imparted. She opened her mouth to protest.

Jack reached out and grabbed her hand. He pulled her behind him, back into his room, releasing her only to pull another white T-shirt over his head. "Come on, if we hurry, no one will even miss us."

In less than five minutes, Laena found herself seated next to him in his luxurious large car, speeding down the back roads towards his mother's house. They reached the lovely, large older home within twenty minutes. He found his key for the front door and let them both in.

Jack looked around slowly, realizing that it truly had been a long time since he had been home. He had a very chic apartment in DC, but it wasn't really a home. He turned as he heard Laena start up the stairs. He followed her and was curious when she walked into his parents' room. He stopped in surprise to find the room completely redecorated. Laena was standing at the long bureau, looking through the drawers, hastily pulling out things. He couldn't believe she was living not just in his mother's home, but was occupying the largest bedroom in the house. That certainly wasn't the way he thought the companion relationship was supposed to work.

Jack saw that the old full-size bed had been replaced by a new king-size one. As he looked around the room, it was obvious that the room had been changed for her. "Why are you in my parents' bedroom?" He couldn't keep the anger from his voice.

Laena turned, her surprise he had followed her evident in her lifted brows and the little "O" formed by her mouth. She brought her hands from the drawer, clutching an assortment of panties and bras. "Your parents' room? Your mother had a room downstairs fixed up for herself the day I moved in. She insisted I use this one."

Jack snorted, revealing his disbelief. "What happened to the bed that was in here?"

"Ruth said it was old and needed to be replaced. She chose all the furniture in here." Laena tossed the lingerie on the bed. "Your mother is a marathon shopper. She wears me out every time we go out for the day." She walked back to the dresser, opening another drawer.

Jack wasn't sure what to make of this woman. He had thought he knew his mother well. Even though she was getting older, she was still completely alert, and pretty shrewd. All this shopping and changing things around didn't make any sense. Suddenly he remembered something that had been bothering him since he'd first arrived at his sister's house earlier. "Didn't my brothers have enough time to help put up Mother's Christmas decorations this year?"

Laena spoke without stopping what she was doing. "Ruth said she didn't want any decorations put up here at the house. I dug out the light forms and a few other things to use at Cindy's house for the big party."

Jack shook his head. "I find it hard to believe that Mother didn't want a wreath or some small things around."

Laena turned to face him this time. "Ask her yourself, but her reasoning was that you weren't staying here, and none of the kids were coming over, so it wasn't worth the effort. I offered several times to buy a tree and bring it in, but she wasn't interested."

Shrugging, he moved over and sat on the bed, watching Laena as she rifled through the drawer once again. He shifted to lean back on his elbows and found he was right next to the pile of lingerie.

Immediately he noticed the rainbow of colors. He realized, with a start, that more than ten years had slipped by since he had been this close to a collection of women's lingerie. He picked up a pair of panties and saw they were cut high on the hips and emerald green. He shook his head as he marveled at the changes since he had last seen a woman's panties up this close. Jack held them up with both hands, and looked at Laena beyond. He looked from the panties, to the luscious curves of her buttocks. From there, it was almost too easy as he imagined what her curvy bottom would look like wearing these sexy panties.

Laena turned to see Jack holding up a pair of her skimpiest panties. She blushed brightly, wondering what he had been thinking. She knew so much about the man lying across her bed that at times she had felt that she had met him long before they actually came face-to-face today. And now, here he was, larger than life itself. He was a man who had political power beyond the sheer imagination of most people. And meeting him now, he was a man who had personal power as well. She had felt the instant attraction to him, and she still couldn't believe what she had felt at his slightest touch.

As she watched him, he slowly raised his eyes and met hers. A slow, sexy smile curved his mouth up on one side, making it even more devastatingly irresistible. Laena felt something inside her melt at that smile. She had been frozen inside for what seemed ages. She hadn't wanted to have anything to do with men, any man, for so long. So why now, when she was finally getting her feet back on the ground, did she have to start feeling again?

Jack felt white-hot, sharp arousal shoot through his body as he met her eyes. He wasn't sure what the hell was happening, but he hadn't felt this horny since he had been a randy teenager. He and Celia had been high-school sweethearts, marrying after he finished law school. All the while, he had never strayed. So, what the hell was he doing being attracted to a woman who obviously was turning his entire family upside-down just by her presence? He dropped the panties back onto the bed and sat up. He saw Laena take a step towards him, and then another. He raised his hand as she came within a foot of him.

Ring… Ring…

A moment passed before they both realized the phone was ringing. Laena turned abruptly away as Jack rolled to the side of the bed to grab the receiver. Laena walked to the closet as she heard Jack say into the receiver, "Oh, Cindy. What? Sorry, I didn't think. We should have told someone we were running over to Mom's for a minute."

Laena listened to his side of the conversation. He had made it sound like it was a mutual decision they come here. She was sure his sisters would be only too sure that he had been enticed over here by her. She knew all too well that Janet and Cindy thought she was up to no good. Though what kind of "no good" she could get up to was still a mystery. She knew the sisters questioned some of the things their mother had been doing of late, but they had all been Ruth's ideas. Laena had pretty much just gone along for the ride.

"In the bedroom? No, Cindy, what are you talking about?"

Laena coughed and choked in the closet at the smooth lie. She grabbed two dresses, and another pair of slacks. She added two blouses, and walked back into the bedroom. She saw that Jack was listening on the phone, nodding his head. He turned as she came around to the bottom of the bed and began folding the clothes.

Somehow, she was surprised when Jack couldn't resist leaning over and picking up one of her bras with his finger. Still holding the receiver to his ear, he looked from the golden satin bra to her face, smiling slowly. Laena reached over and jerked it off his finger, tossing it on the pile. She walked back into the closet and grabbed a small suitcase. Back in the bedroom, she heard Jack saying they would leave in just a minute or two. She had just zipped the bag shut, when Jack hung up the phone. He looked at her, holding her gaze for a moment. Laena grabbed the bag off the bed and started for the door.

Jack sat on the bed a few seconds longer. He rubbed the back of his neck, feeling confused, which was pretty alien to him. He stood and followed her downstairs. As he entered the living room, he saw her glancing through the mail. She set aside the junk mail, but kept a few others in her hands.

"Damn!" she muttered as he saw her read the return address on one of the letters. She folded it quickly and shoved it into her jeans pocket.

Jack wondered what in the mail could have upset her.

She turned and saw Jack standing in the doorway, watching her. Holding the mail in her hand, she grabbed her bag once again. "I'm ready if you are."

Jack checked the doors quickly, and soon they were driving back to his sister's. He couldn't help but wonder what had upset her about the letter she'd shoved into her pocket. He thought back over what Cindy had said on the phone. He had just listened to her vent doubts and concerns regarding Laena, and the fact of her living with their mother. According to his sisters, his mother was spending a lot more money since Laena had moved in. Also the unusual choice for her car, and now she had moved out of the bedroom she had shared with her husband. None of it was making any sense.

"Why is a young woman like you living with an old woman?"

The words dropped into the silence of the car. Finally, Laena turned and looked at Jack. "I needed somewhere to live for a bit, and your mother wanted someone to stay with her. I moved in, and we liked each other. I don't see why you all are having such a fit. What do you think I am going to do?"

Jack didn't know quite what to answer. He knew the reason for Laena being here was a lot more than she just needed a place to stay. Admitting she was a complete mystery, he could tell she was intelligent and well educated. So why would she not be able to support and provide a home for herself?

If his mother's health had deteriorated, why would she suddenly prefer to have a stranger living as her companion instead of moving in with one of her loving children? Every single one of them would have been more than happy to welcome her into their homes permanently. All she had to do was ask—

Laena turned to look out the window at the passing scenery. She knew that Jack's suspicions were just the echo of his sisters'. The letter in her pocket felt as though it burnt through her clothes and into her skin, which was really bothering her. She hadn't received anything from him for so long, close to a year since they'd had any real communication whatsoever. Since she had moved in with Ruth, she had begun to feel that her life was finally getting back onto an even keel. Ruth listened, but mostly she just had brought a lost soul into her own busy life, and kept her busy enough to stop thinking about her problems.

She truly enjoyed her days with Ruth. They laughed a lot, and they could talk about just about anything. For a woman about to enter her seventh decade, Ruth was a woman who took on life with both hands open and eager.

"We're here."

Laena turned to look at Jack, surprised the drive had passed so quickly. She hadn't realized she had been so immersed in her own thoughts, she'd lost track of time. She opened the door and hopped out quickly. Before she could open the back door, Jack had already retrieved her suitcase from the backseat. She wasn't surprised to find Cindy and Janet standing on the front porch.

Jack saw his waiting sisters. He cursed under his breath. The last thing he wanted was a confrontation. Until he had a chance to talk to his mother, he really couldn't take a stand on the issue of Laena living with her.

He smiled and waved at his sisters. "Hey, you two! What did you do with everyone else?"

Jack walked up the steps in front of Laena, thinking to run interference. He saw his sisters both look at the suitcase in his hand. He grinned and decided to cut off their questions with an easy answer. "Laena decided she needed some cooler clothes and since Mom's car was blocked, I drove her over."

Laena grabbed the bag from his hand. She excused herself softly and went inside.

Jack felt his sisters looking at him. He looked from one to the other. He shrugged as he told them, "She seems nice."

Cindy scoffed, and Janet snorted. Cindy folded her arms across her chest, glaring at her oldest brother. "I can see what part of your body you are thinking with, Jack. You men are all alike!"

Jack leaned back, propping himself on the stone balustrade of the porch. He grinned, which only made his sisters angrier. "You know, as your older brother you should know that I am beyond such things, and shall remain impartial." His sisters' snorts of disbelief revealed their opinion of his statement. "I guess you have had this conversation with your husbands."

Janet glared at him. "And Pat, and Michael and Phillip. You men are all alike. You get a busty blonde, and you can't see past the ends of your—"

"Hello, John, dear. Wherever did you disappear to?"

Janet broke off abruptly as their mother called out. All three watched their mother walk up the stone steps of the porch. She came up to Jack and kissed his cheek.

Jack put his arm around her shoulders, pulling her close. "I gave Laena a ride back to your place. Your car is blocked in."

"Oh, really? Why did she want to go back there?"

"She thought she needed some different clothes." Jack saw the doubting look on her face. "She also picked up your mail."

Ruth stepped away from her son, frowning. "All right, dear. I think I will go find her. Did she go upstairs?"

Jack nodded, and then watched silently as his mother went in search of her housemate. He looked back and found his sisters looking right back at him. "What?" he asked in exasperation.

Cindy shook her head, and Janet pointed her finger at him. "We have been waiting for you to get here, Jack, so you could have her investigated. We want her out of Mother's house."

Jack folded his arms across his chest this time. "What do you mean exactly when you say investigated?"

Cindy shook her head and snorted. "You know damn well what we mean, Jack."

Jack laughed. "You can't be serious! You want me to see if there is a Bureau file on her?"

Janet nodded her head fiercely. "Of course. What is the problem, Jack? I'm sure this is an everyday thing for you."

Jack stood and shook his head. "We won't discuss this again. I won't abuse my position. And second, what the hell do you think is going to happen?"

Cindy moved her hands to hips. "Mother has been spending all kinds of money since that woman moved in.

Just look at that ridiculous car! And moving out of her bedroom for the… for her! And now, she has paid to redo the bedroom. It is all too ridiculous and makes absolutely no sense at all, Jack. She is going to get Mother to spend all this money on her, and then leave her in the lurch!"

"Let's just drop it for now. This is the holiday season. Let's just have a good time together." Jack looked from one woman to the other. Finally, they nodded and walked around to the backyard with him. Jack joined in the volleyball game going on, trying not to look at his watch and notice that his mother still hadn't returned from talking to Laena.

Chapter Four

When Ruth walked in, Laena was crying. She had just finished reading the letter she had shoved into her pocket.

Ruth walked to the bed and pulled her into her arms, hugging her. "Laena, dearest, what is wrong?" She patted the younger woman's back, feeling her whole body shaking from her sobs.

Laena sniffed, pushed away from Ruth after a few minutes. She handed her the letter she had received. "It's from Jeff."

Ruth picked up the letter and read its contents quickly. She cursed the man she had known since he was a young child playing with her own sons. Who would have thought he could turn into such a bounder? Ruth had met Laena at the doctor's office. Jeff Hunt returned to practice medicine with his father and her son Michael. Jeff had been working in Richmond, but his father's complaints of ailing health convinced him to return.

And so, he moved back home with his wife, Laena, three years ago. Ruth learned Laena worked hard to put him through medical school, and stood by his side through his internship and residency. And even when he decided to go on and specialize, she still supported him. All the while, he kept telling her their day would come. Once he was established, they would get a nice house and start a family.

Laena believed him, not seeing that after they moved home, he quickly became more distant. Soon he spent longer and longer hours at the office, and seldom wanted to touch her, or make love. A year ago, Laena had been shocked to learn he was having an affair with his office nurse. And the woman was pregnant. Jeff told her he wanted a divorce so he could marry his nurse.

Ruth learned Laena had been stunned at first. Slowly, she realized the signs had been there, but she was just too trusting. Jeff convinced her they only needed one lawyer and they could do the divorce amicably. Laena believed him, and ended up with pretty much nothing. She wanted to move away, but wasn't completely sure where to go. And then, she met Ruth.

At first, they just chatted when they met here or there. And then, Ruth started asking her to do things with her. Ruth wanted to box Jeff's ears for treating Laena so unfairly. She quickly saw how tough things were for Laena, since she couldn't get a job locally as an art teacher. Ruth pretended to have some dizzy spells, and told Laena she didn't feel comfortable being alone. Ruth told her the doctor had given her some horrid suggestions, all of which meant she would have to leave her home. She had shamelessly played on Laena's sympathies, and convinced her to move in with her.

The last three months had been more fun for Ruth than she'd had since her children were little. Laena was a "project" almost. She was watching the young woman blossom once again as she regained confidence in herself. She hadn't planned on telling Laena her plan until Christmas, but decided she needed some good news now. She put her finger under Laena's chin and raised her tearstained gaze to meet hers.

"I have a surprise for you, Laena. I was going to wait until Christmas, but… I'm having a studio built for you in January. We can set up out there and piddle all day long."

Laena frowned, looking distracted.

Ruth hoped that she was forgetting Jeff and the letter he had sent her.

"What do you mean, Ruth?"

"We need a place to do 'our thing'. I'm going to have it equipped with everything you need for your pots, and I am going to start to paint again. I loved those classes we took in November, and I want to do it more often. And knowing you, you would want to be out there with me, or you would worry. This way you can get back to throwing your pots, and making more beautiful things to sell. Perhaps I'll even get two wheels set up, and you can teach me to throw a pot or two."

Laena laughed, smiling at Ruth's exuberance. Warmth, love and concern flooded through her. Somehow, she was sure Ruth was doing this mainly for her, and not because she wanted to paint again. She knew what Ruth's family was going to think. But just then, she didn't really care. She needed something to focus her energies on once again. She missed her work, which she'd given up when she moved out of Jeff's house. She had been crushed when she learned he had sold her wheel and kiln without asking her, shortly after the divorce.

Ruth stood and grabbed Laena's hand. "Let's go downstairs and join in the fun." Her tone told Laena she wouldn't take no for an answer.

Laena was snapped up the minute they reached the backyard to be on the boys' team. She found herself playing on a team with David, Daniel, Chris and John. The other team consisted of Pat, Michael, Hank, Tom and Jack. Tracy and Terry were substitutes for the "dads" team, and Lance and Carl were for the boys' team. Laena tried to refuse, seeing none of the other women were playing, but Chris and John wouldn't take "no" for an answer. Soon she was hitting the ball, playing just about as good as the boys. Once she managed to spike it straight down at Jack. And even though he dove for the ball, he was too late.

Jack groaned as Pat helped him up. His aches and pains weren't helped when he saw his sons picking up Laena and swinging her around, first one and then the other. He felt a punch to his gut as he watched her put her hands on their chests to steady herself. He next felt a sharp stab of jealousy seeing her relaxed and easy manner with his sons. He turned abruptly, stunned to realize he was jealous of his twenty-year-old boys.

Maybe he was having his middle-age breakdown, brought on by facing a career change as well as moving and turning his life upside down. But he was stunned he was feeling this attracted to a younger woman. How much younger was still a mystery, but she looked younger than his youngest sister, Janet, who was thirty-seven. Next to his sons, she looked perhaps a few years older, but he wouldn't have thought by much. Disgusted with himself, he threw himself into the game even harder after that. He dove for impossible balls and tried to slam the ball across the net every time.

The game ended as it started getting dark. The decision had been made to order pizza for dinner, and Jack got roped into driving into town for it. Before he expressed a desire for who should travel with him, his car was filled with his two boys and their two oldest cousins, Chris and John. Obviously, the two younger boys had a case of envy and hero-worship for their older cousins. The twins had changed in the last year since they'd been home. Since he'd agreed to his position at the White House, it was hard to recognize his sons as the same raucous boys they had been.

The car ride into town was a raucous journey with lots of laughter and jostling in the backseat. At one point, things died down and he heard Chris say to Daniel, "I'm in love!"

Daniel laughed, shaking his head. "She is twice your age!"

"So! A lot of women date younger men these days."

David turned around to look at Chris. "You might as well forget it, Chris. Daniel is going to ask her to marry him."

Jack knew they were joking, but his chest tightened painfully with jealousy as he heard. Obviously, they were talking about Laena. He knew how teenaged boys could be. He rationalized that he was being unduly sensitive about the topic of Laena, and he wasn't in the mood to listen to their jesting. Why he should be so interested in a stranger was a question he wasn't ready to delve into right now. The ride back was almost as loud, except that Jack said they could open just one box and have it for the trip home. Eating pizza kept the comments to a minimum.

* * * * *

Laena retired early and was in bed when she heard Jack come into his room. She lay quietly in the dark, listening to the sounds he made moving around the room, obviously getting ready for bed. The bathroom light came on. Soon Laena heard occasional groans coming from the other side of the door. She heard the shower run and then go off. She thought he was almost ready to turn out the light when a soft knock came on her door.

"Yes?" she called out softly.

The door opened and she saw Jack silhouetted by the light of the bathroom. He was wearing a terrycloth robe, open to the belted waist. His hair was still wet, and tousled from being towel-dried. As she gazed at him, her stomach clenched in a gut-wrenching response to his masculine sensuality. She wouldn't have thought he could be more attractive, but with his hair uncombed, she had an intense need to run her fingers through it to restore some semblance of order. And then she would mess it all up again as she kissed him passionately.

"I hate to bother you, but would you have any painkillers?"

Laena smiled in the dark. Undoubtedly, his vigorous play had caught up with him. She tossed back her sheets and hopped out of bed.

Jack watched as she walked over to the dresser top and fiddled with something. He couldn't miss the pajamas she was wearing. While some might call cotton pajamas boring, on her, the super-short bottoms and the crop top were anything but boring. As he watched, she walked back towards him, a small bottle in her hand. Even in the dim light, he could see the bounce and jiggle of her large, round breasts beneath the crop top. Her nipples were hard and made little tents in the material. Jack cursed himself. He was sore as hell, and getting aroused at the same time. *Life really sucked some days*, he told himself silently.

Laena held out the bottle, telling him with a slight smile, "Help yourself." As he took the bottle, she must have noticed the scrapes on his knuckles because she commented softly, "You should really put some ointment on that and perhaps cover it for a day."

Jack shrugged and joked without thinking. "You should see the big one across my back."

Laena paused and then spoke softly, "Would you like me to put some ointment on it? I've got some here." She turned and walked back to the dresser top.

Jack told himself to stop her. He wasn't sure if he could stand to watch her walk back towards him again, and not disgrace himself. But he didn't, and a moment later he was treated to the arousing sight of her jiggling and bouncing breasts once again. He had the fleeting thought that if she had played volleyball in that top—his team would have lost hands down.

He heard Laena tell him to go back into the bathroom and check the scrape on his hand for any missed dirt or gravel under the brighter lights. While he did that, she grabbed a towel and went into his room. When he came out of the bathroom, he saw that she had spread the towel to protect the bed.

She smiled as he came closer. "If you'll lie down here and slip off the robe, I can rub this in for you."

He avoided telling her he was naked under his robe and instead lay on his stomach, and then slipped the robe to his waist. The light from the bathroom dimly lit the room. He felt the bed shift as Laena sat on the bed next to him. She reached over him to where his hands were resting above his head. He felt her soft fingers gently rub the ointment into the scrapes over his knuckles. He wasn't sure if he was just hypersensitive or if he really felt the soft pressure of her breasts against his back as she leaned over.

A moment later, she slowly spread the ointment over the injured skin on his back.

Her fingers felt soft and gentle as she worked in the ointment. After a minute, she was done and put the cap back on the tube. She spoke a few seconds later. "You seem awfully tense still. Um, I could massage your shoulders, if you think that might help. It's probably hard for you to release the tension and pressures you get from your job."

Jack accepted her offer, his voice hoarse in the quiet room. A moment later, he felt her hands begin kneading the flesh at the base of his neck. Her hands worked slowly and methodically across the top of his shoulders and started down his spine, stroking outwards. He could feel his muscles relaxing and tension flowing out of him at her touch.

When she reached his waist, he spoke softly. "You'd think I would know better than getting out there and playing like I was twenty years younger. God! I am going to be so stiff tomorrow."

Laena chuckled lightly, too.

He noticed that she didn't rush to disabuse of the idea of him being too old. A moment later, he felt her fingers snag on the belted robe.

"Do you mind if I loosen this?" she asked him. "I should go down a little bit further, to completely relax the muscles of your spine."

Jack nodded, and then he felt her fingers pulling to loosen the tie. Her skin felt hot against his as she then eased the robe down over his hips. He waited for her to start.

She paused, looking at the tight curve forming his ass and admired his body. She should have stayed in her room, she told herself sternly. But her hands returned to her massage, working down over his hips and finally onto his taut butt. Her fingers curled into the firm flesh, kneading him more deeply now.

Laena wondered at her own intelligence at letting her hands wander onto Jack's firm ass. Oh, my God! He had no tan line! The next thing she knew, she was speaking. "How do you manage to be tanned in the middle of winter and living in DC?"

"Traveling a lot of the time. Occasionally, I can get some time in the sun. What about you? I noticed you are pretty tanned yourself," Jack asked quickly.

Laena had caught him staring at her several times during the day. Since she doubted he was looking for his personal pleasure, she assumed that he must have been wondering about her tan, which was unusual this time of year around here as well.

Laena slowly removed her hands from Jack's warm and supple flesh. The need to continue touching…no, it was time to admit the truth. She'd been caressing his back and pressing not quite hard enough in some places. Massages were something she truly was good at doing, and she knew what she'd just been doing to Jack had nothing to do with a real therapeutic massage.

She had argued with herself several times during the day that being attracted to Jack Spencer was stupid. He was the son of the woman she was living with, and who was also a good friend. The fact he was around ten years older than she was should be a roadblock as well. Most importantly, he lived in a totally different social stratum. They had nothing in common!

She was surprised when Jack turned to his side, propping his head on his hand. He looked at Laena, apparently completely unaware what his robe revealed came very close to indecent. But Laena was completely aware of his naked chest and how much his robe had fallen open to reveal his lower abdomen. She had to close her eyes, and then quickly turned away. She was feeling urges she hadn't felt for years, even while she was married!

"How did you come by your tan?" Jack asked her again, his eyes moving over her tanned legs. She caught his look as she turned towards him again. A definite sexual thrill chased through her body because that look felt more like a sexual caress than a sweeping of someone's eyes.

Laena lifted one hand to push her hair. "Your mother decided to get her hair done twice a week. She had me drive her, and said I was wasting my time just sitting there. Next thing I knew, she told me I was too pale and pushed me into a tanning booth. Your mother can be a steamroller at times."

A moment later, she saw that Jack's gaze had followed the movement of her hand, sliding down her arm. If possible, she felt as if it were an actual caress, the way his eyes caught on the full, lower curve of her breast as her crop top moved with her arm. She told herself she was being a fool but she couldn't stop the way her heart jumped in her chest as she saw his hand moving forward and caressing her closest thigh. His fingertips were just slightly rough as they rested on her skin. She had spent a long time before bed massaging cream into her skin, until it felt like satin beneath her fingers.

Laena's breath caught in her chest as Jack caressed her thigh. It made no sense. She was theoretically "off" men. She hadn't wanted to be near a man since Jeff had first told of his betrayal. So why the hell was this man's touch turning her body to mush? She didn't want to feel all soft and womanly! And she sure as hell didn't want to be aroused by this man! They were strangers and had zero, zip, nada in common. It was so wrong! If anything, he was the last man she should be involved with — he was Ruth's son and that alone made him off-limits. No man in her life was how she had planned the next years of her life. Still, Laena felt her pussy swelling with arousal as he lightly caressed her skin. His fingers skimmed her inner thigh and Laena shivered.

Her mind told her hand to push his hand away. But for some reason, her hand didn't listen. Instead, her hand lifted to caress the back of his hand resting on her thigh. Her fingertips moved slowly over his skin and slid up his forearm. Her hand pressed flat, fingers spread, catching the crisp hairs between them as she caressed his warm skin.

Reluctantly, she lifted her eyes and met Jack's. She found he was already watching her, gauging her reactions. She felt frozen as his hand shifted and moved up over her tummy. He paused just below her full, heavy breast for a second. Her breathing accelerated in anticipation and nervousness. She didn't fear him. Rather it was her reaction to him that made her wary. Never before had she felt so out of control. Her head screamed at her again to get off this bed —

Jack lifted his hand, and sliding it under the loose edge of her top, he cupped her breast in his palm. Her nipple was already hard and he lightly fingered it, teasing it to tighter and longer arousal. As his fingers began a gentle, yet insistent plucking, Laena moaned and her head fell back. She gasped and tried to breathe in more air. But nothing was going to stop the onslaught of arousal crashing through her at that moment. Too lost in arousal to feel the movement, she cried out in surprise as Jack's mouth closed around her other nipple, poking out demandingly beneath her short shirt. Laena's hands moved to the back of his head, cradling him as he suckled her breast, like a man dying from thirst.

Jack was so damned hard with need as he moved closer that he was beginning to think he'd lost all ability to think rationally. An easy movement to lift her shirt and he revealed her tempting breasts to his hands and mouth. When his hot mouth closed over her nipple, he moaned against it a second later as heard the little shocked cry of surprise escaping her parted lips.

He felt the slight pull and tug as her fingers curled into his hair, pressing him closer to her breast. Suddenly, he turned her on the bed to lie flat. He was above her, and resting between her now widespread thighs. In moving around, his robe had come untied, parting completely. Separating his demanding hardness from her wet, eager flesh was nothing but the paper-thin cotton of her pajama bottoms.

Jack groaned, pressing up against her sweet flesh. He breathed in deeply, inhaling the womanly scent of her body. He shuddered with need, overwhelmed by the intensity of his emotions. His body was demanding actions and feelings that he had begun to think were behind him. He moved one hand between their bodies and discovered her pajama legs were very wide cut. The full leg opening made it easy to pull them aside and slip his hand between her slippery, soft folds of flesh.

Feeling her wetness, he nearly lost it. Knowing she was as aroused as he was an incredibly potent aphrodisiac. He moved his fingers up to caress her mound, expecting to discover her bush. He bit back his surprise, and eagerly explored the smooth mound and then equally hairless lips. He slid his index finger between her wet lips and found her clit. His eyes held hers for a long moment. Laena had deep, fathomless eyes like the ocean, and Jack felt as though he was falling into her.

Calling on his strength to contain and control his overwhelming desire and need to hurry, he wiggled his finger around, trying different touches, to discover the ones that made her squirm the most. When he found the one that had her hips jerking rhythmically, he worked her steadily. He gave her no respite. Watching her face as her arousal grew was both beautiful and fascinating. He sensed she was reaching her pinnacle and kissed her open mouth.

Laena's cry broke a second after he covered her mouth, silencing it. But nothing would halt the climax that careened through her body. Her hips jerked and writhed. Her climax came so hard and fast, stopping it, if so desired, would have been impossible. She wasn't aware of her fingernails digging into the muscles of his upper arms. Several minutes later, Laena realized that she was lying on Jack's bed. Her top was pushed above her breasts, her thighs were spread wide and Jack's hand was still resting half on her mound and his fingers lay along her wet, shaven lips.

Perhaps it was a bit late, but suddenly she blushed in embarrassment as she realized how wanton she must look.

She turned her head and found Jack lying on the bed beside her. While she couldn't read his expression, nobody would mistake his physical desire pressing against her hip.

Was she supposed to say something? Her experience was so limited that she really had no idea how to act in a situation like this. Crap! She'd never been in anything like this before. The truth was that other than her ex-husband, Jack was the only other man to touch her like this.

Immediately she realized that never, not once, had Jeff made her feel like this. And she hardly knew this man. That fact was inescapable.

Jack held her gaze as he stroked his fingers along her wet flesh. Her climax had been pretty mind-blowing for him as well as he'd observed it affecting Laena. Even though he hadn't climaxed, seeing her pleasure and knowing he was responsible was pretty heady. Holding her gaze, he slid two fingers into her wet channel. He needed to be inside her, he realized with a start of surprise. He hadn't felt desire this demanding since he was a teenage kid. Emotions this strong were unnerving.

Moving his fingers inside her body, he slid his thumb back onto her clit. He touched the sensitive bud very lightly, and saw how heightened her arousal still was. He lowered his mouth and sampled the succulent delicacies her naked breasts presented him. Her nipples were long and hard, and she moaned as he flicked the taut bits of flesh with his tongue. He moved his head from one nipple to the other. His fingers curved inside her, finding the secret spot deep within her cunt. His thumb moved back to her clit.

The three stimulations were too much. Laena couldn't stop the second explosion inside her body anymore than she could have halted the sunrise. Everything was impossible. She lifted her head and bit his shoulder to stop the loud cry that needed to escape from awakening the household. She thrashed wildly under his touch, and her liquids flooded his fingers.

Jack didn't feel the pain from her bite. He wanted to be inside her and feel her heat around his hard cock. He moved, and was pleased when Laena shifted her thighs further apart. He stopped at her entrance, poised, rubbing against her wet lips and savoring the moment. *God! So damned long since he'd —*

"Hey, Dad? It's David. Are you still awake? I need to talk to you."

Hearing his son's voice, Jack froze. His gaze moved to Laena's and he saw the shock in her face. David's voice had acted like a bucket of ice water thrown over them both. Jack cleared his throat, knowing he needed to say something, or following tradition, his son would open the door and walk in.

"Just a minute, David." Jack held Laena's gaze for a moment and then he rolled off. He grabbed the loose edges of his robe, pulling it together quickly. He looked back and caught sight of Laena's back as she entered the bathroom, nearly running. He heard the door close behind her. He jerked the covers on his bed back up, and walked over to the door. He opened it and smiled at his son. "Hey, David. What's up?" He cringed at his choice of words.

"I need to talk to you about something. Can we go down to the kitchen and grab a snack? I'm starving, too."

Jack grinned and nodded his head. Some things never changed, he realized. No matter how stressed David got about something, he could always eat.

Chapter Five

The first thing Laena did the following morning upon leaving her room was to go in search of Ruth. She found her outside, having make-believe tea with Karen and Kristi. The girls happily invited Laena to join them. She leaned over and asked Ruth to please not tell anyone about the studio until after Christmas. She said she was afraid the announcement would upset everyone, and it would be better to have a pleasant Christmas. Ruth didn't see her point of view, but she did agree to keep it a secret. They then settled back and drank from empty cups and nibbled from bare plates.

Breakfast was a do-it-yourself meal. And after taking her fair share of air, Laena excused herself to go in search of some real food. In the kitchen, she found Pat and Jack sitting at the table, talking over coffee. She stopped, blushing, turning towards the refrigerator quickly. She desperately hoped the brief pause in their conversation didn't mean either man was looking in her direction. Laena had no idea how to handle facing Jack this morning, let alone talking to him again.

"Good morning," Pat greeted her. "Care for some coffee?"

Laena shook her head. "I'm not a coffee person. I'll just have some juice, I think."

Jack spoke softly, yet it sounded like he was right behind her. "You should have more than that. You should keep up your strength."

Laena felt her cheeks flushing even brighter. She hurriedly filled a glass with orange juice.

"Come and join us, Laena. I think most of the family are sleeping in today." Pat stood, gesturing with his hand.

"Uh, all right, Pat." Laena walked over and indicated with her hand that she'd take the seat by the window.

"You should probably slide in with Jack. To keep the ladies happy," Pat added with a sly grin.

Laena realized she had little choice as Jack stood, waiting for her to sit and slide over. Nodding, she complied. "Thank you." To avoid conversation, she sipped her juice.

Pat pushed the plate of flaky croissants towards her, offering her one. Knowing she would be better off just drinking the juice and leaving, she still accepted one and took a bite. She glanced over at Jack and found he had been watching her all along. Hastily, she looked away.

Pat said something to Jack about the transition, and conversation shifted to changes in Jack's life over the next month. Laena listened and learned that Jack was subletting his apartment. Beyond that, he hadn't made a lot of plans. He mentioned a couple of the prestigious, and easily recognized, law firms that wanted him to join them as a senior partner.

She was intensely aware of his gaze lingering on her before he added that he was thinking of moving back in with their mother, for a while, until he sorted things out. Out of the corner of her eye, she saw his hand moving towards her and then he ripped a piece of her croissant away. Without volition, she looked at him, hearing Jack explain that he needed time to relax and slow down.

Laena felt a jolt. She couldn't help but think this decision was last minute. A few times she had questioned that Ruth truly required anyone. But with Jack there, she definitely would not be necessary and once again, she'd be homeless.

Her situation would be different this time. She wouldn't be caught off-guard and she felt a lot surer of herself, all of it thanks to Ruth.

She hurriedly sipped the juice, bending her head and letting her hair fall forward to shield her face. Before she could decide what to do, Daniel and David entered the kitchen. Nonchalantly, they came over and sat down. David sat next to his father, forcing Jack to scoot over and press tightly to her side. Daniel sat next to his uncle. The two young men accepted coffee and eagerly dug into the croissants.

Jack smiled at his sons, proud of them. But he couldn't deny the heat shooting through him as he felt Laena's body against his. He couldn't keep the memories of last night, on his bed, from filling his mind. He was aroused, he acknowledged reluctantly, sitting at his sister's kitchen table with his sons and brother. He looked out the side of his eyes at Laena, wondering if she was as affected by their proximity as he. Half-listening to his sons talk and joke with their uncle, he slid his hand over and covered her upper thigh. He had his answer a second later as Laena jumped and knocked over her juice glass.

Dimly aware his sons were jumping up to get towels, he looked at Laena and found that she was looking at him. No way in hell could he look away. He should move his hand before anyone else noticed. He told himself to do it, but instead he slid his hand a few inches further and covered the apex of her thighs. Laena's eyes opened wide at his bold touch. Jack smiled slightly as he saw the flush staining her cheeks and the sheen of perspiration dotting her upper lip.

Daniel reached over and took her glass while David mopped the juice from the table. Pat clearing his throat drew Jack's attention back to the others. He saw that his sons were taking care of things and then he met his brother's gaze. Pat knew something was going on between Laena and himself. Jack guessed that Pat probably wasn't sure just what it might be yet, but knowing his bloodhound brother, it wouldn't take him long.

Pat spoke a few seconds later. "David? Did you get a chance to talk to your Dad yet?"

Jack was grateful his brother had changed the topic.

Everyone turned to look at David, who flushed under the scrutiny.

Jack saw Pat frown, and he wondered, *what the hell was going on*?

Laena asked quickly, "Should I go? Perhaps you need some privacy."

"No, it's okay, Laena. Everyone else will know soon enough. Daniel knows, and now Dad knows," David told her with a smile.

Pat looked at his brother. "I take it you don't approve?"

Jack shifted on the seat. "I don't know that approve is the right word, Pat. It is just such a shock…"

Daniel spoke up. "Hey, you've always told us we need to do what is right for us. David wants to farm."

Laena glanced from David to his father. She knew from long conversations with Ruth that for many years it had been assumed, planned and finally executed for the two boys to follow their father's law career. She imagined it was quite a shock for Jack to find that one of them was turning towards his grandfather's career, rather than his father's. She could see the stress in David's face. David probably felt he knew what he wanted and was ready to get on with his life. And she had little doubt that Jack's plans had not included one of his sons dropping out of college.

Pat nodded. "David has spent every summer for as long as we can remember working with me on the farm. Daniel always went into town to work. Neither Chris nor John have shown the slightest interest in farming, so far."

David grinned as he looked at his father. "Just look at it this way, Dad. Instead of college, I'm going into the family business."

Laena knew she should stay out of this discussion, but felt compelled to say something. Very gently, she touched Jack's hand, resting on the table.

His eyebrows lifted and mouth opened, revealing how much she'd startled him.

"If you don't do what you love, Jack." Laena moved her fingers, caressing his skin. "Your life will never be happy and fulfilled. You suffer, your family suffers, and your work suffers." She took a deep breath. Part of her wanted to confide her own disappointments, but decided that she didn't know Jack well enough. Nor did she want to lay her troubles at the family's feet. "No one wins. It isn't often someone can go into farming, because so many family farms are disappearing. It's almost like sneering at fate to deny what seems meant to be."

She stopped abruptly, looking from Jack to David. "I'm sorry. I have no right to be butting in here."

David shook his head. "No, really, it's good to have a woman's opinion, and I couldn't have expressed it better, Laena."

Jack looked at his son sharply. For some reason, his son's words made him feel like something even worse was coming. "Why do I get the feeling there is more to all of this than just farming?"

Daniel laughed as David flushed.

Jack looked from one of his sons to the other.

David shifted uneasily on the seat beside his father. He swallowed hard.

A loud noise, which sounded suspiciously like tennis shoe rubber hitting bone, fell into the silence.

"Ow!" David shouted, reaching down to rub his lower leg. The glaring gaze he shot at his brother was unmistakable. A few seconds later, David blurted his news. "I've decided to get married."

If Jack had thought his Christmas holiday had been odd up to this point, this was the final straw. He coughed and spewed out the mouthful of coffee he had just taken. Unfortunately for Pat, he didn't move fast enough. A moment later, he was wearing the coffee.

Daniel started laughing his head off as David slapped his dad on his back. Daniel struggled to his feet to get some more paper towels, passing them to his dripping uncle.

Laena looked from Jack's stricken face to that Daniel, still guffawing so hard that he almost fell out of his chair. She partially stood and drew the attention of them all. "Maybe you two should talk this over in private?" she suggested softly.

Jack scooted to the end of the bench seat and stood. He glared from David to Daniel, and lastly to Pat. "There is nothing to discuss." He reached down and grabbed Laena's wrist and pulled her behind him as he strode out of the kitchen.

Laena had to almost run to keep up with him as he walked through the house, past his gaping sisters-in-law in the living room, and down the front porch.

He kept walking until he reached his car. He opened the driver's side only and tersely told her to get in. She barely cleared the steering wheel when he was beside her and started the engine. A moment later, he backed the car down the drive. He spewed gravel as he sped down the road.

"Where are we going?" she asked him a few moments later, watching him intently.

Jack's hands clenched the steering wheel. "Why?" he asked her sarcastically. "Did you have a prior engagement somewhere?"

Laena looked at him surprise. She scooted over to the far door, glaring back at him. "Just because you don't agree with David's choices doesn't give you the right to manhandle me." She folded her arms across her chest and turned to look out the window.

Ten seconds later, the car pulled onto the shoulder of the road. She turned towards him as she spoke. "Now what—"

Jack turned and reached for her, dragging her towards him. "Damn it, Laena! This is manhandling!" His mouth came down over hers and captured the cry of surprise that tried to escape. His kiss was hot and searing. Jack's tongue took her mouth and claimed dominance.

For a moment, Laena resisted. But just like last night, her resistance was futile, and his touch melted her doubts. She kissed him back eagerly. He was fast becoming a drug she seemed to need.

It didn't make sense, and it certainly wasn't what she wanted in her life right now. She was recovering from the lie her marriage had been. She had no business looking at men, period. There were so many things that she needed time to get her head straight about, not to mention trying to shape her life back together.

Jack moved his mouth down the side of her neck, kissing and licking her tender flesh. His hands jerked her shirt free of her jeans. He shoved up the T-shirt and bunched it under her arms. In the next instant, he dragged down the cups of her bra and her breasts popped free. He cupped a breast in each palm, molding her firm globes with his hands. His mouth opened on the curve of her neck where her shoulders met. He sucked the skin into his mouth and began to tease and lick the skin with his tongue.

With his hands on her breasts, and his mouth marking her tender flesh, Laena squirmed on the seat. "Oh!"

He lifted his head and looked down at her. He took in the dazed look on her face, the obvious red marks on her neck and down to where his hands squeezed and plumped her breasts. The raging need he felt last night came rushing back, on top of the desire he felt now. He heard the gravelly and rough texture in his voice as he spoke. "Tell me what you like, Laena. Do you like sweet words and poetry? What turns you on beyond your wildest dreams? Do you like to be treated like a princess, or shall I tell you what great tits you have?"

Laena couldn't control the bolt of arousal that shot through her as he spoke. As if he had read her mind, he knew instantly what had turned her on so wildly. His head lowered to kiss and suck her breasts. When he finally captured one nipple in his mouth, Laena's cry filled the car. She needed him, like she had never needed a man before in her life. Never had she been this wild with Jeff. Her hands stroked his back and came around at his waistline, tugging at the snap on his jeans. Her fingers had just found the zipper tab, when she heard the slam of a car door.

Chapter Six

Jack glanced up, angry to see who was disturbing them. The next second, he pulled her shirt down with one hand as he snapped his jeans with the other. Two seconds later, they heard a soft tapping on the rear of the car. Jack knew his face was flushed as he turned to look at the sheriff standing just outside his window.

The other man looked surprised for a moment and then a huge grin split his face. "Well, well, well…what do you know? Here I think I've got a couple of high-school kids necking in their daddy's car, and instead I have…well, let's just say something else entirely different."

Jack ignored the other man's knowing grin. "Hello, Howie. Nice to see you."

Howard Striker continued to grin. "Nice to see you too, Jack. Been a while since I've seen you back home. I'd have voted to keep you fellows in another eight years, but the constitution won't let me."

Jack smiled, knowing the other man was a lifelong Republican. "That's mighty nice of you, Howie. Now, when is the next election for sheriff?"

Howie laughed loudly, leaning down to glance into the car at the passenger. His eyebrows shot up and mouth dropped open for about ten seconds, but then Howie quickly recovered. He tipped his hat to Laena. "Nice to see you, Mrs. Hunt. I thought Jeff had told me you were leaving town."

Jack looked at Laena sharply, not liking being kept in the dark, about anything. And he realized that he was pretty much in total darkness when it came to knowing anything about Laena. He watched as Laena glanced at the sheriff and then at him.

"I'm staying in town, indefinitely," she replied softly.

Howie looked at her in a considering sort of way, and Laena knew he would probably tell Jeff he had seen her as soon as he could. The two men were friends, having grown up together. Howie looked between the two of them, and Laena was sure he was wondering if what he had thought he was interrupting had really been happening after all.

Howie cleared his throat and straightened back up. He smiled back at Jack again, jesting. "I'll let you go this time with just a warning, but anymore fooling around—" Howie broke off, flushing as if he decided it was better to just drop it and walk away. "Well, tell your mother hello for me, Jack. And happy holidays to everyone."

Jack thanked him and started the engine. He pulled off the shoulder of the road and headed on towards Ruth's house. A short time later, he stopped the car in the long drive. He didn't open the door, though, just turned to look at Laena. "So, you are married to Jeff Hunt. Why are you living in my mother's house?"

Laena stared out the front window of the car. "No, I am divorced from Jeff Hunt. Why? Are you another lifelong friend of the man's?"

Jack shook his head. "I know him. As kids, he hung around with Michael and Janet mostly. I was surprised when he moved back to town a few years ago. He came back to help his father and Michael in their medical practice, didn't he?"

Laena nodded, frowning. "Yes, the great white savior, returning to the small town with his infinite knowledge and skills."

Jack rested his left forearm on the steering wheel as he turned more to watch her as she spoke. "So, what happened to happily-ever-after in small-town USA?"

Laena laughed harshly, turning to glare at Jack. "Are you trying to be funny? Surely you know—"

Jack shook his head. "Hey, I've been away for basically eight years. A lot has happened. I had enough trouble just keeping up with my family."

"We moved back to town, and Jeff found someone else. End of story."

Jack watched the play of emotions across her beautiful face, in spite of her attempts to keep them tightly under control. He reached out and with his hand beneath her chin, turned her to face him. "If there is one thing I have learned in life, Laena, it is that nothing is that simple."

Laena laughed wryly at herself. "You are right, of course. I was a naïve fool, Jack. I stayed at home, cooked his meals when he deigned to show up, cleaned his house and listened to him tell me the time would come and we would start a family. Unbeknownst to me, he was screwing his nurse at the office. Suddenly he comes home one day and tells me he is divorcing me. His nurse is pregnant and he is going to marry her! I think everyone in town must have known, except me." She turned her face from him.

Jack watched as a tear escaped and slid down her cheek. He stared at her profile for a while in silence. He was still dealing with the kick in the gut he'd felt at the thought of Laena pregnant with another man's child. Why that should matter to him was beyond him just then. And now, to make him feel worse, her tears must signify that she was still in love with the lousy, cheating bastard. Hell! This peaceful Christmas in Virginia was going to hell in a hand basket right before his eyes!

"Are you still that much in love with him that you cry over him?" He nearly shouted the question before he could stop the impulse.

Laena shook her head, turning back and smiling at him weakly. "I fell out of love with him a long, long time ago. I just didn't have the sense to face it until this all happened. You know that letter I put in my pocket at the house yesterday?"

When Jack nodded, she went on. "It came from Jeff. I arranged to have my mail forwarded to Ruth's. Jeff thought I was leaving town and moving back to where we had come from in Chicago, where he did his residency. But I met Ruth, and things worked out differently. Anyway, the letter was to inform me of the wonderful birth of his baby son several months back. Now, doesn't that just take the cake? How many divorced men would bother sending their ex-wives a birth announcement? Surely I'm not expected to send a present!"

Jack shrugged, knowing it was best to not answer and just let her talk and get it all out. He watched as she rubbed her fingers across her cheeks. He wanted to touch her, but he still held back.

"I showed the letter to Ruth yesterday when she came upstairs. When she left me, she said she was going to talk

Michael into leaving their shared practice. She said 'that would teach the little toad'. I can't believe she called him that!"

Jack moved closer, scooting across the seat. His right hand lifted to the seat back, and started stroking and caressing her silky length of hair. He moved his gaze down and realized that in his haste earlier, he had yanked down her shirt, but not righted the cups of her bra. Her breasts were pushed up blatantly against the shirtfront and her nipples were pointed and long. He had to wonder if she had looked like that when Howie had seen them. He shifted closer once again, and raised his left hand to hover above the tempting, jutting mounds. He finally muttered softly as his hand lowered to reclaim possession.

"You are driving me crazy, woman! All I want to do is fuck you, Laena. Is that insane? It makes no sense to me." He pressed his mouth to hers, kissing her openly, wetly and lingeringly. His hand caressed and molded the tempting breasts. He lifted his head after a few moments. "I close my eyes and I see your tits. I can feel how big and full and heavy your boobs are in my hands, even when they are empty."

His mouth sucked on the tender skin at the side of her neck. He didn't care that he was marking her flesh. In fact, he sucked harder, wanting to show his possession. His hand continued to move from breast to breast. Laena squirmed on the seat, rubbing against the ridge of fabric in her jeans. Suddenly, the door next to her opened.

Jack maneuvered around her, and pulled her with him. He had the back door open in a split second, and then she was on her back and he was on top of her, his body firmly entrenched between her widespread thighs. It took him even less time to shove her shirt back up so he could once again look down at her luscious breasts.

Her hands squeezed between their bodies and once again, she released the snap on his jeans, and slid down the zipper. Her hands caressed his hardness before sliding inside his jeans. Her boldness surprised Laena, since she had never been like this with her husband. She quickly shoved that thought out of her head. Everything was different with Jack. It felt new, wonderful and wild!

Laena gasped as Jack returned the favor on her jeans, but he tugged down her jeans over her hips and thighs, to dangle off one foot. She was so hot for him and she couldn't believe this was happening. She had never, ever made out in a car. And now she was about to—

Jack pressed forward, letting his cock rub against her wet pussy lips. It went beyond sweet and erotic, and he was about to go totally crazy with need. His pre-cum mixed with her wetness. His need was overpowering him, making him wonder if he was going to lose control. He groaned as he moved forward, slowly easing into her hot flesh, and wanting to make this as mind-blowing for her as it was for him just then. He looked down at her face and saw she was watching him, her lips parted and she breathed so quickly she was almost panting. His gaze moved down and saw her luscious breasts jiggling with her rapid breathing. He couldn't wait one more minute—

Ring… Ring… Ring…

Jack cursed. Not now, damn it, he thought furiously. This couldn't be happening to him again! The ringing continued and he knew the caller wouldn't hang up. He lifted himself free of Laena's body and leaned over the seat to grab his cellular phone from the holder on the dash. His voice was curt and hoarse as he answered the insistent caller. "Yes?"

Laena flopped back in disbelief and frustration that he had answered the damned phone. Of all the times for a phone to ring! She focused her thoughts on listening to him, and realized it wasn't family calling him. This was obviously something related to his job. Hastily, she yanked up her jeans and righted her bra and shirt. She watched as Jack spoke abruptly into the phone while he jerked closed his own jeans and pulled up the zipper. He went to shift the phone so he could do the snap, when Laena reached out and snapped it for him. His eyes met hers, and Laena was sure that he wished he could read what she was thinking just then.

He hung up a moment later, and turned to look at Laena after replacing the phone. "I have to head back to DC."

Laena was intently aware of the awkwardness in the situation. She looked away from his intense gaze, merely nodding her head.

Jack spoke a few moments later. "There doesn't seem anything appropriate to say at a time like this. Somehow things like 'better luck next time' or 'I'm still hard as a rock, how about a quickie?' just don't seem appropriate."

A laugh broke from her throat before she could stop it. "Neither does 'it's okay' but it is."

"I'll drive you back, and then I'll have to get going pretty quickly."

Jack slid out of the backseat and reached in to help Laena step out.

She didn't want to look at him in case he saw the need that she still felt deep in her body and afraid her feelings might be visible on her face. She climbed into the front seat and sat quietly while he walked around and got in next to her.

He started the car and a moment later they were driving silently back to his sister's home.

Laena was amazed at how quickly Jack was repacked and said his goodbyes.

He lingered with his sons for a bit longer and ended with kissing and hugging his mother goodbye. His gaze met Laena's across his mother's head. He hadn't approached her for a personal farewell. Laena hadn't expected him to. Obviously, he didn't want anyone to know what had happened. She stopped and corrected her thoughts as she watched him climb into his car. What had "almost happened".

A moment later, Jack waved as he reversed down the drive. In the instant before he faced forward to leave, he looked her way one last time.

Laena thought she saw regret in his face, but she couldn't be sure. She regretted they hadn't been able to make love. She had felt an intense and unbelievable need to be with Jack, and the need had gone unfulfilled. She felt empty, alone and lonelier than she could remember being in a very long time.

The car had disappeared down the road and suddenly Laena realized she was still staring after it. She flushed and hoped no one had seen her looking longingly after the disappearing car and its occupant. She turned to leave the porch and saw that Ruth was staring at her. Laena could feel her cheeks getting hotter as Ruth slowly smiled. Before the end of the day, she would be facing an inquisition from Ruth.

Chapter Seven

Laena walked from the studio towards the house, a short distance away. Ruth had been able to get the studio built in record time. Laena's wheel and kiln had been delivered the day before, and she had just spent the morning getting used to working with the new wheel. Each one was a little different and required some getting used to. Ruth had insisted they get a top-of-the-line machine, and it had to be electric and fully adjustable. She had used the excuse that since she would be using it too, as Laena taught her, she would need the comfortable seat, and adjustable levels and foot pedals.

The large oval kiln was going to be perfect, even for the largest of pieces. The clay, both porcelain and red earthenware, had arrived that morning. She and Ruth had a lot of fun mixing up the first batch, both of them ended up wearing more than what got mixed.

Ruth had gone back to the house about thirty minutes earlier, to clean up and start lunch.

Covered in a mix of wet and dry powdered clay, Laena walked along the gravel path to the house. She wore shorts and a white tank top, even though the air was cool today. Working on the wheel while the kiln was firing at the same time was the easiest way to get overheated. It only took one time to faint and pitch forward into wet clay to teach you to take precautions! She raised one hand to push back an errant strand of hair, which dared to drift in the soft air. She looked up and saw someone on the back porch. A few more steps and she stopped abruptly.

Jack stood on the porch, leaning casually against the post, and stared.

Laena couldn't believe that he was here. It seemed crazy that now, the first week of March, he had returned. He had been technically unemployed since January twentieth, and she was surprised when he hadn't returned home earlier as he'd talked about at Christmas.

She did not need to listen to his sisters and sisters-in-law talk about how he could have any woman he wanted, rich, beautiful and well-connected. In fact, his youngest sister had pointedly told her that if he found the right kind of wife, he could possibly run for president himself. Without asking, Laena realized she had learned what Jack's plans for his future truly were. Power such as he'd experienced would be heady and hard to walk away from.

A divorcée without a dime to her name would hardly make the right kind of wife for a politician. Of course, the difference in their ages would be fodder for the gossips. Not that she cared —

Many sleepless nights she'd wondered if he'd doubted his actions those few days, wishing they'd never happened. Could he have stayed away, fearing she'd assumed his actions were a commitment he had no intention of following through?

Suddenly she had to take a deep breath to steady herself. The pull of attraction was still hot and fierce. At times over the last three months, she wondered if it had all been her imagination. But no, it was still there, in full force, just waiting for the slightest bit of encouragement or for her to relax her control, and she just might be jumping his bones in say fifteen or twenty seconds.

Gasping at her wayward thoughts, she continued walking towards the house.

* * * * *

Jack had learned from his mother Laena was out back in the studio. He had heard about the "infamous studio" over the last few months from his sisters' weekly phone calls. He had spoken to his mother and told her he liked the idea. Their mother had loved painting before her marriage, and she never had time after he came along. If building it on the excuse it was for someone else would get her back to painting, then he was all for it. That opinion had not pleased the ladies in the family.

The temptation was strong to rush back after he closed his office, but the paperwork had taken longer than he had anticipated. And then, he had been invited to visit the former president's home. He spent a week with other staff people they had come to know well over the last years. The trip was intended to serve as sort of a goodbye and thank-you celebration, allowing them all a real closure, since many had been together for eight years.

Following that week, he had returned and spent the last two weeks packing his belongings so his apartment could be sublet, until he decided where he would go with his career from here. He had already received enough invitations for speaking engagements to keep him busy for the next nine to twelve months, at least. And those engagements always paid well, not that he had to worry about money any time soon.

He had wanted to give himself some time. That had been his original plan, once their term in the White House ended. Since his visit home, he definitely wanted to spend more time with his sons, especially since David had not returned to school after the Christmas holidays. He felt bad about not getting a chance to discuss David's decision before leaving. Their phone calls since then had been brief, but at least he hoped they had healed any lingering wounds.

The brief time with his family at Christmas had merely highlighted the fact he needed to get reacquainted with his entire family, and mend a few fences that had suffered due to his job and busy lifestyle the last eight years. Meeting a woman and developing a light companionship had seemed a possibility, but it had always been on the edge of his thoughts. He couldn't say that he was opposed to the idea of a relationship, but he assumed he would never remarry. His sons were now grown and had no need of a stepmother. Perhaps he was old-fashioned, but he could see no reason to marry because he had no intention to have more children.

By no means did he plan on doing without sex. Now that he was out of the public eye, and he believed he'd reached the age when compunction would no longer be a factor, surely no reason could be found for him to forego the company of a mature woman.

Laena was not at all what he'd planned on, though. She didn't fit any mold or type he'd previously known. Everything about her screamed knockout, and judging by the reactions of his sons and nephews, she'd have no trouble attracting a man of any age or wealth she desired. Why was she attracted to him? Hell, he was almost…hell! He was older, but he didn't know by how much.

And now, standing on the porch and watching Laena walk towards him, he knew that what he'd felt at

Christmas had not been a figment of his imagination, nor an exaggeration caused by time. Her arms and legs were bare, but spattered with clay and dust. She looked worse than his mother had when he surprised her thirty minutes earlier. Laena had a streak of dried clay across her forehead and on one cheek. Jack could see her white T-shirt was dotted as well as her jean shorts, but that didn't detract from the beauty of her body.

He could see her full, unbound breasts jiggling as she walked across the rough path. He thought briefly that he would make sure the path was taken care of and fresh gravel brought in to make it smoother and much less muddy. But his main thoughts were occupied with remembering how beautiful she had looked on the backseat of his car, with her naked breasts and her hot, slick pussy ready to welcome his hard manhood into her body.

Jack pushed away from the railing. Oh, yeah…these feelings were real, hot and needing to be acted on—soon. He grinned at Laena, and walked down the couple of steps towards her. Being quite ungentlemanly, he told her baldly, "Someone looks like she played in the dirt. Your mud pie partner is taking a bath."

Laena blushed and walked the last few steps, coming up beside him. She felt the intense physical pull as she stood next to him. His masculinity swamped her as he stood there, looking so average in his jeans and white T-shirt, and yet he was so very far from being average, that it was ridiculous. She unconsciously lifted her hand to push back her hair once again, but this time Jack caught her wrist and stopped her. Startled, she met his gaze.

"I think you have enough war paint on already," he informed her with a smile.

Laena blushed hotly as she realized that she must have been smearing the clay each time she had pushed back her hair. She lowered her arm. "If you'll excuse me, I was going to rinse off before going in the house. I want to get a hose attached at the studio, but we have been too busy to do that yet."

Jack didn't release his grip, continuing to hold her gaze. Instead, he pulled her with him towards the side of the house, where the hose was hooked up. He turned it on, directing it at her. "Kick off your shoes and I'll rinse you down."

Laena looked at him for a moment, and then reluctantly did as he commanded. Stepping closer, she braced herself for the cold water.

"Turn around, Laena. I'll start in the back."

She turned and gasped a moment later as she felt the water hit the backs of her legs. It didn't take long and she faced him again.

He rinsed the front. Slowly he moved the nozzle over her legs, working down.

She held out one arm to be rinsed, and then the other. When she cupped her hands, he let the water fill them and she rubbed until they were clean as well. She briskly rubbed at her cheeks and forehead, closing her eyes.

A few seconds later she screeched as the water hit her upper chest, where she knew she had some dried bits of clay. In only a few seconds, she was drenched, her white tank top plastered to her naked skin. Her nipples were hard and tight, and poked at the clinging thin white cotton. She looked down at the blatant display. She heard the water hose hit the ground and looked up.

Jack took the last step and stood right in front of her. His hands lifted and she had but a moment before they covered her breasts possessively. He groaned when she rubbed her hard nipples against his palms. His hands squeezed her large breasts, and then rubbed his palms in little circles over and around the taut centers.

Laena leaned into his touch, offering her breasts more fully to his hands. She looked up into his face, and saw his clenched jaw and steely-eyed gaze. She had no doubt that his need matched hers. Her hands slid up over his chest and cupped the back of his head. Jack offered no resistance as she pulled his head towards her open mouth. She kissed him hotly and her tongue entered his mouth, seeking his heat.

Jack moved his hands around her body and dragged her close, pressing her into his chest.

It felt hot, sweet and erotic to feel her wet upper body pressing into his. Her fingers curled into his hair, which was longer than before.

Jack moved one hand down to her bottom and cupped one cheek. He pulled her hips into his and pressed his hard manhood into the soft cleft between her thighs. There was no mistaking that his need was just as strong as before.

Jack moved his hand from her buttock. It slid around slowly, his fingertips caressing the skin exposed under the short jeans, moving forwards. Once he reached the front of her thigh, it was only a second longer before he slipped his fingers between the gaps of short jeans onto the naked flesh below.

He froze. "Damn, woman! You aren't wearing any panties!" He could feel her wetness on his fingers, and it made him harder and hotter than he could have thought possible. His fingers slid along her wet, swollen pussy lips.

Laena told him breathlessly, "There is a couch in the studio."

The words had barely left her lips, and they were almost running along the short path towards the studio. Jack slammed the door shut behind them and pulled her into his arms. He lowered his head and kissed her deeply. He looked up a moment later and sighted the couch. He moved them over to the long, extra-wide sofa. His hands took a moment to cup her full breasts beneath the wet material. He realized in an instant that she felt sweeter and sexier than she had just two months earlier. Nothing really important had changed!

Jack tugged her shirt over her head, throwing it aside. Her jeans were next, but he did pause for a moment to stare at her lovely body. Off came his shirt, followed by his shoes. Before he could move his hands to the snap on his jeans, Laena's hands were there.

Laena yanked on the snap and slid down the zipper eagerly. Her hands pushed at his jeans and jockey shorts.

Jack had but a scant second before he felt her eager hands caressing and stroking him. He had really wanted to make this first time last, but he was becoming resigned to that not happening. Of course, considering their false starts in the beginning, he should be grateful they were getting as far as this!

Laena stepped backwards and lowered herself to the sofa. One leg was on the floor and the other was bent at the knee. Jack gasped as he looked from her full breasts, quivering with her rapid breathing, down to where her body was spread open for his taking. He groaned and lowered himself. As his hard cock pressed forward, she encircled his hips with her legs. She pulled him closer, and then the head of his cock slipped past her outer lips. They both groaned together as their flesh joined.

Her eyes closed, savoring the feel of his heat, so close to her, finally.

"Laena, open your eyes."

Slowly, she looked at Jack.

He held her gaze as he pushed forward, entering her body a millimeter at a time.

She rocked her hips upwards.

Jack could hold back no longer. With a groan of defeat, he thrust.

Laena felt him sliding in and out of her body, shifting position.

He slipped one hand between their bodies.

She gasped as he began to tease and torment her supersensitive clit. Her hips thrust up to meet him, and she lifted her arms around his shoulders. She pulled him close as her body shook and trembled, and in the next instant, her orgasm engulfed her. She cried out, needing him to —

"Fuck me, Jack!" Laena gasped, surprised at her own words.

She met his eyes and saw the heat rise a few more degrees. She smiled as he began to thrust into her eager body more quickly.

As if spurred on by the trembling muscles squeezing his cock, he came hard and fast. His body jerked, and he filled her with his seed. Over and over, he thrust into her wet heat, until he finally collapsed on top of her.

Laena listened to his raspy breathing, and slowly noticed the feeling of heat deep inside. She realized it was the heat from his body being truly inside of her, and now she would have some sweet reminder of him within her —

Jack shifted above her. He eased out reluctantly, but rearranged them on the sofa to lie face-to-face. He stared into her eyes, wishing he could read her thoughts just then. He leaned forward and kissed her lips lightly, fleetingly.

Laena smiled slightly, feeling drowsy and sated. She closed her eyes, and let her body curl into Jack's.

He closed his eyes, not pausing to wonder why he felt so amazingly relaxed and at peace. Jack awoke to the sound of the old triangular dinner bell being rung. It took him a moment to realize that he and Laena had fallen asleep. He rubbed one hand across his eyes, and then turned his wrist to look at his watch. He was surprised to see that almost two hours had passed since his arrival. He looked down at Laena and saw she still slept soundly. He wondered if her nights had been as restless as his. He couldn't count how many times he had awakened from an erotic dream starring Laena. This last hour or so was probably the most solid sleep he'd had since Christmas.

"Hey, sleepyhead, time to wake up," Jack murmured softly, leaning over her ear. "I think my mother is being discreet. She just rang the dinner bell for lunch."

Laena opened her eyes, meeting Jack's. She smiled.

He wondered if her smile was related to what they'd been doing earlier.

"Does that mean we don't have time for a quickie?" she asked with a wink.

Jack laughed out loud. That was probably the last thing he would have expected her to say. He levered himself off the sofa. He saw his jeans next to the sofa and stepped into them. He slid on his shoes, and then glanced around for his shirt and her clothes. He turned back around a moment later, expecting to hand them to her.

Laena was still lying on the sofa, on her side, facing him. Her head was propped on a bent arm, and her top thigh slid forward and down just enough to conceal her mound.

He had to groan. With her blonde hair disheveled, Laena would have made the perfect centerfold picture just then. Jack shook his head and walked back over to her. Reaching down, he took her hand and pulled her to her feet.

"You have no idea how much I wish my mother was somewhere else right now."

Laena grinned and then stepped into her jean shorts. She took her shirt, but it was still wet.

Jack grimaced and passed her his shirt. "Put this on."

Jack grabbed her hand, not allowing Laena the time she would have liked to just savor the warmth and smell of his shirt. They walked hand in hand up towards the house. When she saw Ruth standing on the back porch, Laena wiggled her hand, trying to free it from Jack's firm grip.

But he wouldn't release her, even as they started up the porch's stone steps. He smiled at his mother. "I was trying to help Laena rinse off when I got her shirt wet. I offered her mine in exchange. She was just showing me your new studio. I look forward to seeing some impressive works of art coming from there soon."

Ruth smiled at her oldest son. "Well, come along inside, both of you. I just made a quick lunch for us. I thought we might go out to dinner to celebrate your return, John."

Jack nodded his agreement and released Laena's hand to open the door for the two women.

They enjoyed a leisurely lunch and conversation. Instead of returning to the studio after lunch, Ruth announced her plans. "Feel free to go back to the studio, Laena. I'm going to straighten the kitchen and then take a nap." Turning and starting the water in the sink, she told Jack, "Go with Laena and help her finish setting up the studio. That will keep you out of my hair and the house quiet so I can sleep."

Jack smiled at his mother. "Always glad to be the dutiful son, Mother."

Ruth glanced over her shoulder at them both, her eyes going from Jack's blue shirt—which he'd donned prior to eating—to the white one of his Laena still wore. "In case anyone shows up unexpectedly, you might want to work on an explanation for the interesting pattern on the shirt."

As Ruth resumed her work, Laena looked down for the first time. She felt her cheeks flushing brightly as she saw the quite distinctive red clay design on the white shirt. There were two small hands at the shoulders and two distinctive circles partially covering her breasts. Obviously, she was not as clean as she'd thought. When she lifted her head, she saw Jack was smiling.

He didn't wait for her comment. Without pause, Jack grabbed her hand and trotted back outside.

Chapter Eight

They made their way back to the studio. Wandering around the outside first, Jack checked the structure for soundness and construction errors. Finally, stating he was pleased with the workmanship, they walked inside. He followed Laena around the room asking her questions, until they came to the sofa.

Laena couldn't stop the blush that covered her cheeks. And almost as if Jack read her thoughts, he smiled. She turned to walk away.

Jack reached out and pulled her back. He swung her around and into his arms. As he pressed her close to his chest, his strong arms held her tight while he looked into her upturned face.

She could feel her full, soft breasts mashed into his chest. Glancing upwards, she met Jack's gaze.

"No regrets, Laena," he murmured to her gently.

Laena frowned not completely sure what he meant. "I'm not sure I understand you, Jack. Do you mean that you have no regrets about earlier, or are you questioning if I have regrets?"

"I have no regrets, Laena, and I hope you don't either."

Laena couldn't stop the rush of joy she felt at hearing his words. "I have no regrets. Well, maybe one."

Jack froze, not liking the feeling of trepidation he felt at her words. "What do you regret, Laena?"

Laena moved her hands to rest on his chest as she looked up at him.

He noted how serious she appeared.

"I regret that we didn't get this done at Christmas."

Jack laughed and kissed her smiling lips. "On that point, I agree, honey. I knew that no one else but the President would have been calling me that last afternoon. He is the only one who had that number. I had to answer."

"I know. I missed you after you left," Laena told him softly. "I barely knew you, but it was obvious to me—"

Jack frowned as she paused. "Go on, sweetheart. What was so apparent to you?"

"That you were gone. A hole was where you were supposed to be."

Jack shook his head, frowning. "I doubt it was much of a spot, Laena. I've been around my family and they can fill in the Grand Canyon with noise and activity."

Laena leaned back, getting a better look at his face. "You wouldn't see it, because you are there. But I saw your family before you came, and on several different occasions, remember? Then I saw how things changed with you present…it was different."

Jack was surprised, and more than a little embarrassed at what she had just confessed. He wondered if her honesty had taken her aback as well by the way she suddenly looked away.

With one finger beneath her chin, he tilted back her face. Jack lowered his head to kiss her softly. "You have no idea how much I missed you. Laena, you are the first woman I've been with since I lost my wife. I don't want you to think what happened at the holidays was just a need for any woman. I have had plenty of opportunities and offers. I just was never interested. God knows why you should be the one…" his voice trailed away. "I don't mean that you aren't beautiful and attractive," he added hastily.

Laena laughed. "I know, because I was thinking and feeling the same thing." She pressed closer and wiggled her hips against his hardening manhood. "Like right now. I think we are both feeling this couch must be used again—"

Laena screeched as Jack turned with her in his arms and dropped onto the couch, with her landing on top of him. His hands were already unsnapping her jean shorts, and pushing them off her hips. Her hands tried to return the favor, but he was too fast for her. Kicking his shoes off, he quickly pushed his own jeans down and off. He lifted her to straddle his hips, and his hard manhood stood proud in front of her shaven mound.

Jack's voice was tense and hoarse as he spoke. "Take me inside your heat, Laena. Use your hands and make us one."

Jack growled as he watched her gaze move up his body.

Her hands pushed up his shirt and caressed his chest, circling his nipples, and rubbing them with her fingers. Slowly, as she moved them down his body, she tangled her fingers in the curls above his manhood. Meeting his gaze, she tugged on the curls and smiled. "You know what I want to do?"

Jack groaned as the thoughts of possibilities swamped his consciousness. He barely managed to croak out, "What?" Then he felt her soft hands on his body.

"I want to make you as smooth as I am. I don't know what you will think of me for saying this...but I've always wanted to feel a smooth cock sliding in and out of my pussy, and feel our smooth skins brushing against one another. I've wondered what it would be like to suck smooth skin." She curled her fingers around his manhood and began caressing the soft, velvety skin of the head. Her hips were rocking back and forth as she straddled him, caressing her flesh with each forward and back movement.

"Damn!" Jack caught his breath at her words. He had dreamed often of her smooth, hairless mound. The dreams, not to mention the daydreams, had driven him nearly to the edge of control at times. His daydreams were filled with images of him sampling her womanly delights and checking her smoothness for perfection. But it was at night, deep in slumber, it wasn't her sweet, hot pussy driving him crazy. Wild and unbridled were the dreams of her mouth sucking his cock, his balls, spending long moments inspecting her shaving technique.

The erotic thoughts were almost too much to handle, along with her sweet caresses. He looked at her now and saw her moving forward, rising on her knees. She held him, until her body was in the perfect spot. He watched as her thigh muscles relaxed, and Jack could feel the pressure as her flesh eased and parted, until the head of his cock popped inside her body.

She didn't move for a long moment, just letting the feelings and sensations overwhelm her as he slowly filled her.

Jack's hands came to her hips, wanting to complete their union.

Laena pushed them away. She grabbed his wrists and lifted his hands to her breasts instead. Her lips curved upwards in a small smile as she whispered, "This should keep your hands busy." She let her thighs relax slowly as she felt his hands close on her full breasts. As her flesh swallowed his cock, she began rocking her hips.

Jack shoved up her shirt and began caressing her naked breasts. His squeezes on her large, round breasts matched the rhythm of her rocking.

Laena had to grab hold of his forearms to steady herself as the sensuality swamped her senses. "Dear God!" she cried out as he plucked at her nipples.

But he slid his hands to her waist, supporting her body. "Lift your hands behind your head."

Laena did as Jack asked just as his hands began to control the rocking of her body. The position lifted and pointed her breasts upwards. She saw that Jack's eyes were watching the enticing jiggle and sway of her heavy breasts. Her voice was hoarse and shocked her as she spoke. "Tell me what you see…like…"

Jack smiled, more of a grimace. "I love your big tits, Laena. They bounce and jiggle as you move and it gets me hard just watching you. My fantasy is to make love to you, and fall asleep suckling your nipple. And when I awaken, I start all over again, with your nipple already in my mouth. I'll suck your nipples until they are long and pointed. I'll suck them hard so when you pull free, we both hear the erotic wet plop of it coming out of my mouth."

Laena cried out at his words. Her body responded on the most elemental level, and her orgasm rose through her. Only his hands at her waist kept her fully seated.

He paused, watching her head roll back as his words washed over her. He could feel her body responding to each erotic word he said. "Shall I tell you my second fantasy?"

Laena gasped, barely able to whisper, "Yes."

"I want to come inside you, and stay there, keeping you plugged so none of my seed can run out. And then, I will fuck you again, and again, until every move you make has my seed leaking from your flesh all day long. All day, until I take you back to bed and we start all over again."

Laena gasped and tensed as the vision of what Jack said materialized in her head. She groaned, unable to delay the climax that swept over her in the next second. Her body jerked and his hands tightened to hold her secure. She ground her hips down and rubbed her clit against him, and she came again.

Seeing the climax overwhelm Laena was almost as gratifying as coming himself. Almost…He held her hips firmly and his pelvis moved beneath her, thrusting into her wet flesh. He came hard and fast, which wasn't surprising considering the pulling and tugging on his cock by her cunt muscles. He felt as if her body milked his cum as she spasmed repeatedly.

Finally, his hands slid up her body to cup her breasts, just as she fell forward to lie on his chest. Jack moved his hands to her back, holding her close, as they both lay there in the silence of the afternoon.

They savored the feeling of aftershocks coursing through their own, and the other's, body while still so intimately connected. She rubbed her cheek on his upper chest enjoying the soft curls tickling her cheek.

Jack soon heard her soft breathing become slower and deeper, indicating that she had once again fallen asleep.

Sometime later the ringing of a bell awoke Laena. She lifted her head to see that Jack was asleep still, and their bodies were still joined, as in his fantasy. She shivered as the sensuality of it all swept through her. She whispered his name.

A smile was curving his lips as his eyes opened. He lifted his hand to tangle in her hair and pull her close for a soft kiss. And then, the bell rang out again.

"Damn!" Jack cursed. "Of course, I guess this is better than her coming down here to find out how we've been filling our time."

Laena blushed hotly and struggled off his body. She found her shorts and slipped them on quickly.

Jack moved more slowly, sitting on the couch for a few moments. "Just watching you get dressed is a turn-on, sweetheart. Your big boobs sway and jiggle with each move you make. All I want to do is reach out and grab on, holding tight."

Belatedly, she remembered and yanked her shirt, or rather his shirt, back down. She looked around and saw his jeans. Picking them up, she tossed them to him.

Jack dressed more slowly, tucking his shirt in lastly. He held the door open, muttering as she walked past him, "I just hope she doesn't ask to see what we've been making out here."

Laena gasped and glared, which earned her a light slap on her derriere as she passed him. She was tempted to stick her tongue out at him, but resisted and walked towards the house, hearing Jack close the door and follow her. She had just entered the kitchen when she saw Ruth sitting at the table, which had a view of the large backyard, including the studio's front door. She flushed, but sat at the table and accepted the glass of iced tea Ruth pushed towards her. She was sipping the tea as the door swung open again to admit Jack.

Ruth watched Jack's gaze go from her to Laena, lingering.

"Good afternoon, Mom. I hope you had a good nap." Jack grinned as he took the glass of tea she held up, leaning back against the sink counter.

"I had a lovely long snooze." Ruth nodded. "It reminded me of the early days of my marriage to your father before you came along. Many times he and I enjoyed a lovely nap after our dinner." Ruth smiled, looking from Jack to Laena. "I rang the bell to let you know we have an hour to get ready before our dinner reservations." Ruth told her son and the young woman she was coming to love as a daughter, hiding her smile behind her glass of tea, sipping slowly. Things were progressing much better than she could have hoped for.

Chapter Nine

The drive into town was filled with talk between Jack and his mother, who insisted on taking the backseat of Jack's car. They were all dressed in their finery, which gave Laena the first chance to wear the new dress Ruth had insisted on buying her a few weeks back. Being black was the only thing simple and understated about the dress. It was high-necked, and fit almost like skin to her hips, where it was draped and caught in a sexy rhinestone clasp that rested on her right hip. The material ended a few inches short of her knees, and was slit partway in the back, to allow easier walking.

Other than clasping around her neck, no material appeared again until the very small of her back, where the skirt began. She had added the velvet thigh-length jacket in deep red that Ruth had insisted she buy. Laena questioned the red color, but Ruth had pointed out that the rhinestone clip was clear and red stone, so it was a perfect match. And sometimes, it took too much energy to argue with the older woman.

Laena was surprised when Jack pulled up outside the only expensive restaurant in the area. The real shock was that Ruth had gotten reservations at the last minute like this.

The parking attendants opened their doors, and Jack walked between the two women as they entered the restaurant. As the maitre d' greeted them almost obsequiously, Laena guessed Ruth did some major name-dropping to get their last-minute reservations. Evidently, Jack was a favored son of the town, because of his former position.

They were shown to a lovely table, which wasn't in the least secluded. As they were seated, Laena caught the wry look Jack shot his mother. He was obviously just as aware of what Ruth had done, as she was. As he turned from his mother, he caught her gaze. As he smiled slowly, sensuously, his gaze told her he remembered their times earlier in the day.

Their waiter gave them menus, and Jack ordered a bottle of wine. After sitting for a few minutes, Laena became too warm to keep the velvet wrap on any longer. She tried to slip it off and then put it over her shoulders only.

But Jack was too quick. He stood and moved behind her to remove it all the way.

As he folded the jacket over his arm, he glanced down and saw the bare expanse of skin now exposed. "Holy shit!" Jack said in surprise.

He looked away and found his mother watching him, grinning. Without a doubt, his mother knew about the surprise beneath the coat. Frowning as his thoughts raced through his head, he shook them off.

"May I check madam's coat?" The waiter returned, offering politely.

Jack looked at Laena. Even as he noted the bright flush that stained her cheeks, he saw her start to shake her head. Emboldened and feeling naughty, he grinned and handed the coat to the waiter. If he had to suffer, then so would she, he decided with a soft laugh.

Ruth lowered her head and covered her grin with a sip from her wineglass. As she looked up though, she couldn't stop the gasp of chagrin. Across the dining room, yet only about four or five tables away, sat her son Michael. He was not alone. He and his wife were having dinner with his partner, Jeff Hunt, and his new wife, and former nurse, Arlene. Jeff's father Frank had also joined them.

"Oh my!" Laena said quietly.

Jack turned to look when he heard Laena echo his mother's surprise. He recognized everyone at the other table but the one woman, who he quickly assumed was the "nurse in Jeff's office". He muttered a succinct, "Damn it."

Laena's pale face concerned him. He saw his mother had covered Laena's hand, which rested on the white tablecloth. Leaning forward, he heard her speaking.

"Do you want to leave?" Ruth asked, keeping her voice low-pitched.

He watched as Laena turned slowly. He stared intently, until her gaze met his. Their eyes held for a moment.

Then she moved on to Ruth. "No, I'm fine," she whispered, shaking her head. "I was bound to see them sooner or later if I stayed around. We both knew that."

Jack looked at the other table, glaring. Unfortunately, that was precisely when Michael decided to look around the restaurant.

His brother's raised eyebrows, followed by his smile, revealed his surprise at seeing Jack seated a few tables away. Michael waved his hand, motioning for Jack to come over.

Jack realized that from Michael's viewpoint, Laena was blocked from his field of vision, and probably Michael only saw their mother and himself.

He groaned out loud, not wanting to deal with this confrontation. All he wanted was to savor the warm and wonderful feelings still lingering from earlier in the day. And he had had every intention of continuing their reunion tonight in her bed. Before he could respond, Michael apparently said something to the others because he stood and began walking over.

Jack whispered Laena's name a second before Michael reached their table.

The look on Michael's face changed from joy to dismay as he saw Laena. If there had been any doubt, his muttered "damn it" would have proclaimed it.

Ruth admonished her youngest son. "That's no way to greet your family, Michael."

Michael flushed, and hurriedly looked at his brother for help.

Jack guessed Michael had told the others he would ask his mother and brother to join them, and now he was stuck on what to do.

Michael pulled out the extra chair and sat heavily, propping his chin on his fist. And being Michael, he just blurted it all out. He had not told Jeff that Laena lived with his mother, either, which he knew would not go over very well.

"Damn, I've really screwed things up now! I just told them I would ask you to come over." He paused and looked at Laena. He liked her, in spite of his sisters. He saw the improvement in their mother since Laena moved in. "I'm sorry, Laena, but I didn't see you were here as well."

Laena smiled at Michael. "It's all right, Michael. This was bound to happen, after all, this is a pretty small town."

Michael nodded and turned to Jack. "Well, have any brilliant ideas, my diplomatic brother, to get me out of this mess?"

Jack shook his head, turning to look at Laena. "What do you want to do? We can leave, if you want."

"I could take just Mother back and say you had a business call, or something."

Ruth shook her head, patting her youngest son's hand. "Thank you, dear."

Michael grimaced, but shrugged. "I'm sorry, but I never told Jeff Laena had moved in with you."

Ruth chuckled softly. "Oh, really. So, he doesn't know?"

Michael shook his head, reaching out to sip from Ruth's glass of water. "No!"

"Don't fret, dear. It isn't entirely your fault. Jeff's father has known all along as well. Quite obviously, he has kept quiet. You know, I'm not surprised about Frank, though. He never has liked confrontation."

"And Arlene knows how to give good confrontation," Michael murmured. Immediately he realized what he said and looked at Laena. "Damn! I'm sorry, Laena. I shouldn't have said that."

Laena was still dealing with the warmth that rushed through her at Jack's consideration of her feelings. He would do what she needed. She blinked quickly to clear the unexpected moisture from her eyes. She shook her head. "It's all right, Michael. I thought it was rather funny, actually."

She shifted her hand and squeezed Ruth's. "We can join them, if you two would like? I am okay with this, really. And I would kind of like to see the shock on Jeff's face."

Aware that Jack stared at her for a long moment before turning to his mother, she smiled.

Ruth shrugged, indicating it was up to Laena.

"All right, let's go slay a few dragons, shall we?" Jack said decisively as he signaled the waiter, telling him they would be joining the other table. Standing, he indicated for Ruth to follow Michael, and he and Laena would be right behind them. He held her hand for a moment, letting his mother and Michael arrive first. When he saw the questioning look in her face, he grinned. "I have learned that timing *can* be everything, my sweet. I'm right behind you."

Laena nodded and stiffened her spine.

They had nearly reached the other table when Jack whispered, "Don't get too far ahead, honey. Watching the swaying back and forth of your pretty little ass is making me hard and horny."

Laena couldn't stop the gasp at his words. She stumbled slightly and immediately felt his hands at her waist, catching her.

A moment later, he pressed close. His arm wrapped around her waist. They were a foot from the table, and everyone talked between one another, welcoming Ruth. Jack cleared his throat.

Laena waited tensely for the others to notice them.

Frank Hunt stood as soon as he saw Ruth walking over with Michael. He'd always had warmth in his heart for Ruth and all she had overcome, since she'd lost her husband, raising all those kids. Lately, he had even begun to notice how damned attractive Ruth was. Since he'd lost his own wife a few years earlier, many women had considered him fair game but he'd not had any interest in anything beyond his practice.

Several times he had tried asking Arlene about whether she thought he should start dating once again. Times like that made him realize how much he missed Laena as his daughter-in-law. He'd always been able to stop over for coffee and talk.

Arlene was too snooty for his likes. She hadn't been that way in the office. But after she'd married Jeff, Arlene made it well known that she was now a member of the "country club set". Jeff cared about image and money, but he couldn't care less.

Now, looking at Ruth Spencer, he found a new interest in dating, and women. No, not women in general, he realized with some surprise, just Ruth.

He kissed Ruth as he hugged her close. "You look lovely, Ruth."

Ruth flushed. "Why, thank you, Frank. You're looking pretty nifty yourself."

Frank started to reply when he noticed another woman had joined them, and she stood in front of Jack. It only took him a moment to take in the arm around her waist before he glanced upwards and realized the woman was his former daughter-in-law! Quickly he glanced over and saw that his son was equally surprised, which was to say nothing about the look on his new daughter-in-law's face. Hiding his chuckle, he came forward. He'd never been a man to waste time on what other people thought so he reached out and pulled Laena into his embrace. "Why, Laena, my dear, what a delightful surprise!" But he did decide to maintain his air of ignorance. "When did you get back into town?"

He had quickly decided to pretend he had not been the one to suggest Laena as a companion to Ruth. No good would come from that knowledge, or at least not right now.

Before Laena could answer, Ruth spoke as she held his gaze. "You told me I needed a companion in the house, Frank, *remember*? And Laena needed somewhere to live, so we made a bargain."

He recognized Ruth's reminder of a conversation they'd had some while back. Hopefully the subject would drop here, and later he could explain to Ruth his thoughts on the bending of the truth. Frank nodded, and held out the chair for Laena. Reluctantly, he went back around the table to resume his seat next to his new daughter-in-law. In his unvoiced opinion, Arlene's only redeeming point so far was that she had given him a grandson.

Frank looked at Jack, who had taken the seat next to Laena. It appeared Jack had been staring at Jeff. Remembering the arm around Laena's waist, Frank imagined Jack must have been gauging the ex-husband's thoughts and emotions. That's what he would be doing.

Clearly, Jeff's new wife was angry, considering the glare towards Jeff at seeing her husband's ex-wife appearing here instead of being a thousand or so miles away. But Frank guessed the only thing Jack cared about was whether Laena still had any feelings for the ex-husband across the table.

With Michael and Frank seated on the ends of the table, that left Sally, Laena and Jack now seated opposite Ruth, Jeff, and Arlene. Needless to say, tension was thick at different parts of the table.

Jack shook Frank's hand. "It's nice to see you, too, Frank."

Sally looked at her brother-in-law. "What are your plans now, Jack?"

Jack shrugged. "Nothing, to be honest. I've thought it over and decided to take some time off. If the money runs out, I've got a couple hundred offers for speaking engagements already."

Michael laughed. "You! Run out of money? Not bloody likely, bro!"

Jack shrugged and looked at Laena. "One never knows what you can find to spend your money on these days. Some things are more expensive than others." Very purposefully he looked at Jeff, slid his gaze to Arlene, and finally again at Laena. With intent, he laid his arm along the back of Laena's chair, curling his hand around her far shoulder.

He ignored the glare from Laena as he glanced around the table. His mother barely concealed a grin behind her glass of water. He had half-expected a dirty look from his mother, but was coming to realize his mother might have her own plans in mind when she had Laena come live with her.

Frank coughed and choked. As everyone turned in his direction, he cleared his throat. "I'll call over the waiter and let's order, all right?"

Laena thought she'd be nervous, sitting across from her ex-husband and the woman he had divorced her for.

But Jack kept her mind, and her responsive body, too occupied to have the energy to notice much else. His fingers kept moving to caress the naked skin of her back, and every so often, moving up to the nape of her neck.

She'd worn her hair up, into a soft, sophisticated chignon. Several shorter hairs had fallen down. Jack let his index finger catch one of the trailing strands, and idly curled it around his finger, before finally releasing it slowly. The very intimate gesture sent shivers up and down her spine. She turned her head the first time he did it, to admonish him. But instead, she found herself meeting his intent gaze, and the words died on her lips. It required Frank's insistent voice to draw her attention back to the general conversation at the table.

She saw the looks that Arlene kept shooting at her husband. She couldn't help but guess that the other woman assumed Jeff had known his ex-wife was still in town. If it had been her, she'd be ticked Jeff had not objected to eating dinner with his ex-wife. She had wondered why, out of the blue, he had notified her months after the birth. Many things hadn't made a lot of sense.

Arlene spoke loudly. "Sally? I know you can appreciate this with three children of your own. Little Franklin is walking already. We are—" she paused and covered Jeff's hand where it rested on the table, "—so proud of him. Jeff pointed out that he did this nearly two months earlier than normal."

"Oh. Congratulations, you two!" Sally complimented Jeff and Arlene. "Uh, do you have a picture?"

When Jeff didn't immediately reach for his wallet, Arlene elbowed him hard in his side. Jeff pulled a picture from his wallet and passed it across the table to Sally.

Since Laena was seated next to Sally, it was impossible not to see the baby's picture. She smiled at the giggling baby's picture. Above the roaring in her ears, she heard Frank saying something about the baby, and turned to compliment him on his attractive grandson. The words died on her lips as her gaze collided with Jack's. She saw the concern on his face. She smiled at him instead. Moving her hand to his thigh, she pressed it lightly, to reassure him. Keeping her hand there, she looked across the table at Arlene. "He is a lovely baby. Congratulations to you both!"

When Arlene had brought up the subject of the baby, Laena guessed she struck out in the only way possible in this public venue. She wouldn't blame her if she were pissed at not knowing the ex-wife was still around. Possibly, it was her way to point out her claim on Jeff. *Then again*, she thought with a smile, *maybe she was just a proud mother*.

Jeff and Arlene both looked at her in surprise. That was something neither had probably expected. Laena turned back to look at Jack, and impishly gave into the need to squeeze his firm, muscular thigh. She felt the jerk of his muscles in surprised response, and the look he gave her promised reprisal.

Jack finished eating first, probably from too many years of rushing through state dinners and dinners on the road, never knowing when he might be interrupted again. He noticed the small live band starting a short time earlier, remembering the dance floor in the lounge section. He pushed out his chair, drawing everyone's attention. He clasped Laena's hand as he excused them to the table. "Laena promised me the first dance." He ignored the surprised look on her face and pulled her to her feet. He led the way to the floor, letting the full effect of her dress be absorbed by the people left behind at the table.

On the floor, he pulled her close and slid an arm around her, while the other held her hand. He easily matched his steps to hers. His hand began sliding down her naked skin until it rested in the very small of her back, at the curve of her buttocks. He pressed her intimately against himself, letting her feel his hard cock, which had been present for a good portion of the evening. "How are you doing?" he asked, whispering into her ear.

Laena pulled her head back, surprise evident by the look on her face. "I'm fine, actually, much better than I thought I might be. I'm glad it's over, the first meeting, that is."

Jack nodded, but lowered his head to kiss the side of her neck. He sucked the tender skin and quite deliberately marked her flesh lightly. He licked the abused skin afterwards, and met her gaze as he looked up. As if reading the question she didn't speak, he told her, "I'm marking you as mine."

He grinned when Laena gasped. He knew he pushed the envelope for sheer macho chauvinism in his statement. But for some reason, he didn't care. It felt good to claim Laena as "his woman". When she didn't say anything, he pulled her back into his tight embrace, matching his steps to hers.

Back at the table, they found Ruth had ordered a small cake to welcome Jack home. He smiled tightly, wanting to excuse himself and take Laena home. Instead, they all had to have a piece of the cake. Jack cut off a small piece of his and picked it up in his fingers. Calling her name softly, he watched until Laena turned. He barely allowed her the time to open her mouth to prevent having cake all over her mouth. Jack smiled, liking the intimacy of the act.

Even more, he enjoyed the astonished look on Jeff's face before he could hurriedly look away. He smiled the whole time as Laena returned the favor. Only he caught her hand and held it while he licked off the clinging bit of icing. He felt the frisson of desire that chased along her nerves as his tongue stroked her skin. Fully aware of the sexuality of their little food play, he did wonder if Laena was equally tuned in to vibrations generated around the table.

Jack wiped his mouth with his napkin and announced that he was dead-tired following the long drive, so he thought they would call it a night. He glanced over at his mother expecting her to stand also as he pulled Laena to her feet beside him.

But Ruth just smiled at her oldest son and spoke gently, "John, dear, you two go on home. I'm going to stay a bit longer. Michael has offered to give me a ride home." She smiled complacently.

Michael found himself nodding and ignoring his wife's surprised look.

Frank looked at Jack. "You run on home, Jack. I'll be more than happy to see your mother home."

Ruth flushed as Frank turned back and smiled at her. *My goodness*, she thought to herself, *I'd forgotten how good-looking Frank Hunt really was!* She nodded her head and slowly released the punished hand of her son.

Jack didn't need any more encouragement. He excused them, and without allowing Laena any time to say anything other than goodnight, they headed out of the crowded dining room. He quickly retrieved her coat, and they drove back to the house.

Chapter Ten

Laena looked at the speedometer on the car and was surprised they didn't run into the sheriff again.

Jack literally sped all the way back home. He didn't bother parking the car in the garage. Once inside the house, he pulled her close and covered her surprised mouth with his. He finally pushed her away, but only for a second. Grabbing her hand, he started up the stairs at a near run. Inside her bedroom, he locked the door. Then he grinned. "If it weren't so chilly tonight, I might have risked pulling off the side of the road again."

Laena smiled back, glad to see his thoughts had been the same as hers.

Jack was already tossing his jacket, tie and shirt to the side, even as he kicked off his shoes. As he got a few steps closer, his hands were undoing the belt and his trousers soon followed in the same direction, narrowly chased a second later by his brief jockey shorts. He jerked off his socks, balancing on one foot at a time.

Laena watched as he kept getting closer and more naked each passing second. And then, he was right in front of her.

He turned her and gently unfastened the clasp on her dress at her neck and waist. As she turned back to face him, his hands dragged the dress down the front of her. He growled low in his throat as he looked at her naked breasts. "I've been going crazy since I realized you didn't have any kind of bra on under that damned dress tonight!"

Laena gave him a fake smile. "So that means you don't like my dress after all, then?"

Jack shook his head. "It isn't good for my blood pressure." His hands were already pushing her dress past her hips.

It fell into a pool of black at her feet. By the harsh breath Jack took, she guessed that he wasn't prepared for the fact she had on no panties and was left wearing a black garter belt, decorated on the lace with red roses, black stockings and her black heels.

"Damn it!"

Laena looked up into his face. "What's wrong?"

Jack threaded his fingers into her hair and pulled the pins from it. He pulled it forward to drape over her breasts. "If I live through the night, you just may be the death of me."

Laena frowned and shook her head, not quite sure what he meant.

It didn't help when he smiled gently before adding, "They will put on my tombstone, 'Fucked to death by the most beautiful woman in the world'."

Laena blushed at his exaggerated praise, but was warmed by it also. "Lucky for you I know CPR."

Jack laughed, pulling her into his arms. They fell to the bed in a tangle of arms and legs. "I like a woman who is always prepared."

"I guess that means I'd have made a good scout as a boy, right?" she asked him, giggling while she kicked off her heels, eagerly slipping her silky legs up and down his.

She was already wet and needed him inside her body. She kept surprising herself by her demands. For a woman who had been happy living without sex, she was suddenly turning into a sex maniac. She rocked her hips against his hard cock, pressing forward to let it slide along her wet lips. He pressed against her clit with the velvet over steel rod, and she felt the shivers shoot through her body.

Jack looked down into her smiling face. He wanted her. He needed her. More than anything, he desperately needed to be inside her. He thrust forward and felt her legs lock around his hips. There were no slow, gentle movements this time. Hot, fast and hard. His thrusts were quick, jerky and needy. He wanted to hold off and…it was too late. He climaxed and shot his seed deep into her body. The spasms rocked his body with their fierceness. He groaned, half in embarrassment for not seeing to her needs first. He fell to the bed beside her, breathing harshly. Finally, he turned to look at her, not sure what he would see on her face.

Laena smiled as he opened his eyes. She reached out and lightly caressed her fingers over his lips. "I didn't know that chocolate cake could be that powerful an aphrodisiac."

Jack laughed, shaking his head. "You are the aphrodisiac, honey." He took a deep breath. "I'm sorry—"

Her fingers pressed his lips, stopping his words. "No apologies. I don't have a score card, I'm not keeping track." She caressed the side of his face. "Although on the rating scale—" She squealed as Jack rose, pushing her back flat to the bed.

Looming above her, he growled and tried to look fierce. "Rating my performance, are you, wench?"

Laena laughed. "Yup. I'll give you an eight, out of ten, that is."

"Eight!" Jack frowned intentionally.

Laena reached up and pushed his hair off his forehead. "Now if I were rating this afternoon? I'd give you—" She paused and looked into his face as if she were truly thinking it over. "Hmmm, I guess it would be fifteen." She nodded her head. "Yup. Fifteen all the way."

Jack lowered his head and kissed her gently. His hand slid down her body, between her breasts and onto her smooth pussy. He caressed her with purpose, and sureness. As if he had been pleasuring her for many years, his touch was skilled and deft. Her hips squirmed as he worked her clit unrelentingly.

She shook her head, murmuring quietly, "You don't have to do that, Jack."

Jack looked into her beautiful face. He did have to do just this exactly. Something deep inside cried out to witness once again the look of passion that flooded her being as it had earlier today. "I was a member of that scout group, my sweet," he told her patiently, as if that explained everything

Laena gasped when he slid his fingers inside her cunt. He watched the pass of emotions across her face as he wiggled around until he found her G-spot. Soon he massaged it while his thumb continued to bring drowning pleasure through her clit.

"So, I am your duty?" she asked him a moment later, in between panting breaths.

"No," Jack spoke quickly, and stopped his fingers for a moment.

Laena opened her eyes and met his intent gaze.

Quietly he told her, "You are my joy." Without releasing her gaze, he began to move his fingers against and inside her body once again. He had no idea how long he continued to caress and pleasure her.

Her climax seemed to come from nowhere, without warning. His first signal came when she bit his shoulder, suppressing her scream. Then her head fell to the bed, and she panted hard. Her heavy eyelids lifted, looking up at him.

Jack continued smiling, and his hand started once again, giving her tender, eager clit no respite. This time, he slipped three fingers inside and curved them. He kept his thumb busily teasing and working her clit, even though the wild squirming and jerking of her hips threatened to part them. Easily he found the spot within her body again, and his fingers pressed it insistently. He massaged the flesh within her, and didn't remove his thumb.

Her body went wild once more, losing complete control. She screamed this time as her body climaxed in the ultimate act. She jerked and moved fitfully, even as her fluids soaked his fingers and hand.

Jack felt her muscles spasming deep inside her body, even as her hips jerked.

Time passed, and Laena had no idea how long it had been before she opened her eyes. She immediately became aware of two things.

The first was Jack above her, still smiling and watching her. And the second was that his hand rested tenderly and possessively over her mound and pussy lips. She could feel the heat of his hand and the wetness. It was a heady experience, for sure. She took a deep breath and he lowered his mouth to kiss her lightly, tenderly. Slowly, his hand moved up her body, her flesh drying his fingers and hand as they caressed her body.

She was limp and drained.

Jack moved and covered them with the heavy comforter. He pulled her into his arms, her head resting on his chest.

Above her head, she heard him yawn as he flicked off the bedside light. Beneath her cheek, she could feel the heavy, steady beat of his heart. She was gently lifted and lowered with each breath he took. Just as Laena was sure that Jack had fallen asleep, she felt him caressing her hair with one hand, taking a deep breath and preparing to fall asleep.

Maybe it was silly, but Laena realized that she had never felt this comfortable before. Certainly, she'd never been this satisfied with Jeff. Hell! She'd never really been satisfied period during her marriage. Quickly she pushed her ex-husband metaphorically out of her bed. The only two people she wanted in here were Jack and her. Shifting around so she could look up into Jack's face, she then stared at him.

Finally, he opened his eyes. "Yes?" he asked softly.

Laena shifted off his chest and rolled over onto her side, propping herself up on her bent elbow. "I thought you would want to know."

Jack smiled, looking bemused.

Grinning, she knew he wouldn't be expecting her next comment. She winked slowly. "I just gave you a new rating." She stopped, knowing she had his complete attention now.

"What is it?"

Without answering right away, she turned away. Flopping onto her back, she settled onto her pillow and interlaced her fingers as they rested on her abdomen. "I assume you want the full rating."

"Of course," Jack muttered next to her.

A quick, sideward glance told that he was smiling. "For the performance by a middle-aged athlete—"

"Middle-aged! Hey!" Jack interrupted immediately.

Laena felt the bed shift as he moved.

A moment later, he was on his side, looking down at her.

"The judge meant no offense, sir," she told him with a smile. "If anything, pure appreciation for the athlete's perfect body and his ability—"

"Perfect?"

Laena stopped to grin. "Certainly in comparison to other specimens of similar age…but this is only a distance kind of rating. The judge has very limited intimate comparisons to base this on."

Jack's finger pressed against her lips a second later. "The athlete fully understands because he has very limited experience as well."

Laena met Jack's gaze through the darkness, disturbed dimly by a small night light. To Laena, everything this man did was perfect. The comfortable feeling just moved from that sweet, satisfying place, plus humor, into something else. She wasn't sure that she could go on with the silliness because of the growing knot in her throat. Swallowing hard, she told herself that to do anything else at this point was unacceptable. She went on with a saucy wink, "Um, the judge awards you a twenty, sir."

"Twenty!"

Laena could hear the surprise in his voice, even if she couldn't still see his face as clearly. Nodding, she added softly, "At least."

She was surprised as she felt the bed shifting again and realized that Jack was lying back down beside her. What she'd expected him to do she wasn't sure, but it wasn't this. Several long moments later, she heard him breathe in deeply.

"A hearty thank you to the judge, but the athlete wonders if a medal is included in this rating," Jack asked her quietly.

She couldn't hold back the giggle that bubbled forth. Perhaps it was joy at the way he played along with her nonsense and didn't get upset or fall right to sleep after telling her he was too tired to talk. "Yes, the judge does have a medal for the athlete, but she doesn't have any pockets at the moment—"

Laena gasped in surprise by the way Jack reacted so quickly. In less than a second, he was sprawled half across her body. Two of his fingers were already delving deeply past her wet pussy and up into her hot body.

Her body reacted instinctively and hopefully by jerking her hips and tilting them to fully receive his touches.

"I do believe the judge is lying. Yes, here it is. I was sure that I remembered a pocket of some kind." Jack grinned down unrepentantly.

Since her body had already been primed by two orgasms, it didn't take long at all for his clever and very adept fingers to stimulate her to one more. There were several things she wanted to tell him, but she fell asleep immediately as the last shiver coursed throughout her entire system.

Chapter Eleven

Jack awoke during the night, and rolled over to pull Laena close to his body. His hand found nothing but an empty bed next to him. He moved his palm over the cool sheets beside him. That meant that she had been gone for a while. He turned back to his side and rolled out of bed. He flipped on the light and then walked back to his room, finding a pair of jeans, cotton shirt and shoes to put on. He wandered downstairs, heading to the kitchen first. But the kitchen was dark, so he got a glass of water, while he wondered where she had gone. He leaned against the sink, looking out the window.

He noticed a faint light coming from the studio. Jack drank all of the water, and then as quietly as possible, let himself out the back door. Upon reaching the studio, he opened the door, allowing only one squeak.

Seated at the wheel, Laena worked the clay with her hands. She was forming a tall, slender vase. Abruptly, she pounded the clay flat with her fist.

Jack then noticed the tears running down her cheeks in the dim light. He didn't want to consider that she might be crying for what she had lost. Maybe seeing Jeff that night with his new wife had made it all too real once again. He had to know if that was what she thought. No way could he go back to the house, possibly lying in the dark, unable to sleep, and wondering if Laena now regretted making love to him. He cleared his throat.

Laena looked up. "Jack! I didn't want to wake you."

He moved across the studio towards her. "You didn't. I reached out and you were gone."

Laena nodded. "I woke up and needed to do something. I couldn't sleep. I felt restless and I decided to come out here and test the wheel."

Jack nodded slowly. "Why did you smash the vase?"

"Huh?" Laena looked at him. "I didn't like the way it was thrown."

Her confusion at his interest was apparent on her face. "But why the tears? You can't be that emotionally attached to the pot already, can you?" Jack prodded her further.

Laena laughed. "I smash a hundred pots for every one I end up finishing. Tears?" She paused and rubbed the back of one hand against her cheek. Glancing at the wetness, she shrugged. "I remembered how you made me feel today, and I guess I was crying for lots of things. Lost time, mainly. I don't know, Jack. Probably it is just too much emotion for one day, after months of feeling nothing. Or at least, months of trying to keep my feelings and emotions at bay finally caught up with me. To be perfectly honest, Jack, you rather overwhelmed me today."

Jack grinned. "Babe, you swamped me totally."

Laena smiled. "Guess we surprised each other, huh?" She pounded the clay as she spoke. "I think I could go back to sleep now. Can you open the container over there?"

Jack helped her clean up, putting away the clay and rinsing down the wheel. They walked up to the house, and Jack used the hose to once again rinse the clinging clay from her body. Inside he toweled her off with one of the spare towels kept there. Finally, they headed up the back stairs. In the bedroom, Jack suggested they take a quick shower to warm up.

Laena nodded and stripped off her clothes in the bathroom.

Jack adjusted the temperature of the water. He stepped back to let Laena step into the shower first. He dropped his own clothes to the floor and came in after her.

Laena let the water splash down over her head, using her hands to push her hair back off her face. Smiling, she turned to face Jack.

He pulled her close, and stood with her under the warm water spray. Their slick bodies rubbed against each other.

Laena was unable to resist the lure. She moved her hand down, between their bodies. She threaded her fingers into his pubic thatch. Looking up at Jack, she tugged at the hair lightly. "What do you think, big fella? Are you up for a shave tonight?" Immediately she felt his body jerk in surprise.

Jack groaned at her joking words. "Honey, any time I'm around you, I seem to be *up*."

Laena laughed. "Then your barber is ready."

Jack saw the eager expression lighting her face. Any doubts and misgivings he might have had faded as he met her gaze. He followed her out of the shower, and then he went in and lay on the bed, placing a towel down first. He watched as she reentered a few minutes later, carrying an assortment of things.

She pulled the nightstand closer to the bed, and set up her array of supplies. She turned on all the lights. "I want to be able to see really well. After all, I wouldn't want to cut off something important, or even something I might care to use later."

His body had an immediate reaction, jerking slightly.

Laena grinned, her gaze darting away.

He looked at her quickly. The mirth and enjoyment she was having at teasing him was evident by the look on her face and the sparkle in her gaze. Something tugged in his gut, deep down. It was an emotion he had not felt in more than a decade. This was more than lust or passion. Tenderness and the kind of stuff that pulls at the heartstrings… Quickly he pushed it away because he felt uncomfortable and strange when it involved his heart.

Jack had thought his emotional life—his feelings for his children and family—was complete. Anything else he might feel would be lighter and less serious and sexual, naturally.

He certainly felt lust, passion and never-ending arousal whenever Laena was around, and even when she was not. Letting these other feelings creep in wasn't in his game plan—

Laena touched one of his legs as she seated herself on the bed, between his widespread thighs.

Her touch drew his attention back to the present. He'd propped his head on two pillows so he could see what she did more easily.

She picked up the small scissors and clicked the blades a few times. As her gaze met his, she lifted one eyebrow and asked, "Last chance to change your mind!"

Jack shook his head and watched.

Laena lifted a tuft of hair on his lower abdomen and snipped it off. She lifted the sandy hairs and playfully let them drift over his flat stomach.

Jack once again shook his head at her.

But she continued to snip off the pubic hairs on his lower abdomen. Once she finished there, she moved lower, and snipped the few long ones on his cock. Her hands were very slow and deliberate as she clipped the hairs on his sac.

"How many times have you done this before?" Jack heard the words and realized that he'd spoken his thoughts out loud. Cursing himself for revealing his vulnerability, he waited anxiously for her reply.

Laena paused and looked up. "This is the first. Do you want me stop?" She down set the scissors. "From this point, it wouldn't be hard to let it grow back. Or at least, not so itchy."

"What happens now?" he asked, not sure if he considered stopping her for real or not.

Then he felt her fingers brush off the stray hairs, including the ones she had playfully scattered across his stomach. He couldn't stop the shiver of reaction as her fingers rubbed over the stubble she had left behind.

She looked up at his face. "Now I use the electric razor to clean up, so to speak. Next, I will wet your skin with the warm water, apply the shaving cream and begin."

Silence seemed to hang between them over the next few minutes. Finally, Jack held her gaze as he whispered softly, "I trust you."

She picked up the rechargeable razor and flipped it on. Holding the razor in her hand, she moved it to his lower abdomen and began shaving the short hairs left by the scissors. She moved the razor slowly, wanting to cut the hairs as close to the skin as possible, without causing any razor burn.

Jack shivered as her fingers caressed his skin after the razor passed over it.

After several minutes, she turned off the razor and checked the skin carefully for stray hairs.

Jack took a deep breath and wondered if this was as far as she intended to go. But the next moment, he saw her filling her palm with white, fluffy shaving foam, and he knew more was still to come. He watched as she slowly smeared the shaving cream around his skin. She took her time, and Jack guessed that she needed to make sure she coated the stubble fully.

She wiped her fingers on the small towel before she picked up the razor. Very carefully, she placed the blades against his flesh and stroked it across his skin. Over the next few minutes, Laena focused totally on what she was doing. And Jack was consumed by the feeling of her gentle hand touching his skin, pulling, tugging, moving her fingers to straighten his skin and make it easier to reach.

He groaned as one hand tenderly held his cock while the other used the razor to carefully shave away the miniscule stubble. And when she came to shaving his sac, she had to push and tug on the skin to straighten the wrinkles. After that, she rinsed her hands and spent a very long time running her wet fingers over his sac, checking for missed hairs.

Finally, she bathed her hands of any remaining foam. The next several minutes were spent checking every millimeter of skin she had just shaved.

Jack groaned as her wet fingers caressed and tantalized him unrelentingly. When she finally removed her hands and announced "done", Jack was sure his torture just might be over. He was dimly aware of Laena setting things aside. He lifted his head from the pillow, expecting her to say something else.

Laena, though, continued sliding down the bed, still between his spread thighs. She told him to lift his hips, and she pulled the towel from beneath his hips.

His hips settled back onto the bed.

Laena's hands clasped his hard cock.

Immediately his body stiffened in shock.

Laena had opened her mouth and taken the head of his cock into her mouth.

Surprise continued to rattle his nerves on top of his rising passion.

She sucked on his cock, and her tongue touched the joining of flesh at the back of his penis, which formed the rim at the base of the head. Her head bobbed up and down quickly, letting her lips catch and pull on that sensitive rim of flesh.

Jack felt boneless and lay helplessly against the pillow.

She paused and her tongue licked around his hardness. She stopped at the back, the joining of the rim, and her tongue moved quickly and repeatedly against the sensitive spot, like a small, hot, wet whip. Her tongue slid down the back of his cock and when she reached his sac, she drew his hairless, wrinkled skin into her mouth. She stroked her tongue along the ridges, and then pulling the flesh into her heat, and rubbing the skin against the back of her teeth.

Jack groaned as he felt every sensual tug as a bolt of lightning-hot arousal. And when she sucked one of balls into her mouth, Jack clenched his fingers, forming fists.

She released his flesh and cupped him in her hand. Her hand began rolling his balls within the sac of now hairless flesh.

Jack was amazed at how much more intensely the touch of her fingers, her tongue and her mouth felt upon his body.

Laena felt aroused simply knowing she was able to pleasure this man. She had never done anything like this before. She had read several books, and lots of magazine articles, all in hopes of finding what was needed to spice up her marriage. But the one time she had tried something adventurous, Jeff had looked at her as though she was something dirty. But lying in this bed with Jack, she felt different. She felt beautiful, desirable and wanted. And now she needed to give him pleasure as he had done for her. And if this were all she could have with Jack, she'd take it… eagerly.

Her mouth caressed his shaved belly with gentle kisses. She moved her hand down between her thighs, and wet her finger with her juices. She proceeded to surprise herself, and Jack, as she circled her finger around his pink, wrinkled hole. She felt the shock ripple through his body at the unexpected touch. She paused for a moment, waiting for him to reject her.

Instead she soon felt arousal stirring once again. Never in her life had she ever made love more than once a day. And the once a day had been on her honeymoon, and not once since then. Maybe she was a repressed sex kitten.

Jack couldn't believe what Laena had just done. The light touch, teasing, circling and not quite entering his body was erotic beyond his realm of experience. His hands moved to her hair, clenching in the soft, long strands. He tried to form words, but his throat had closed. All he could do was groan as he felt her finger once again circle and tease around the supersensitive flesh she had found there.

She lifted her head from his belly and looked up at his face.

He could only guess what she saw.

Seconds later, he felt her mouth moving back to his cock, and then she licked all around the rim with her tongue. As her mouth shifted above him and sucked him into her mouth, she entered his body with her finger.

God!

Gently exploring, her finger moved inside, wiggling around. The last thing he expected was for her to find the place...his breath stopped as she pressed, prodded and massaged.

"Oh God!" he shouted, unaware of time and lost in his own pleasure. His exclamation heralded the moment he erupted like a volcano into her mouth. He came so hard, liquid dribbled out of her mouth. His hips jerked and rocked on the bed.

Laena's mouth slipped from his cock and the last spurt of cum hit her face and dribbled down onto her right breast. She slid her finger from his body and grabbed the nearby towel. She washed her finger in the water, and proceeded to wipe the drops from her face and breast. She climbed off the bed and turned off all the lights. As she returned to the bed, Jack lay unmoving. She pulled up the covers and climbed in beside him.

Jack turned his head to look at her.

Laena paused, feeling that something was different in the way he saw her. She stiffened and wondered if he had been disgusted by what she had just done. She couldn't voice her fears and doubts as tears clogged her throat all of sudden. For so long, she had listened to all the negative things Jeff drilled into her over the years of the marriage.

Maybe it was silly, but this was something she'd never told anyone. So many times, Laena would try something new, and Jeff's reaction was always negative. She tried new recipes, new furniture arrangement and even a new dress style. Every single time, Jeff would shoot her down, and he never did it kindly. After awhile, she blamed herself and believed she was too vulnerable and sensitive. But if Jeff could be cruel to her verbally, he seemed to relish the opportunity.

At the end of their marriage, she had felt like a kicked puppy. Not only had he been systematically humiliating her within their home, he had been publicly conducting an affair. When she went to the office after receiving the divorce papers without forewarning, Jeff had introduced her to Arlene, who was pregnant, telling her it was her fault.

It didn't matter that she had no basis to assume Jack would think the same. She had felt relaxed enough to fulfill a fantasy for herself, but had she so appalled Jack that he now wouldn't be able to—

Her mind stumbled over using the words. No words of emotion had passed between them. He hadn't said he cared for her, and certainly the "L" word had not been mentioned. She turned away from him abruptly, rolling over in the bed. She pressed her hand against her mouth, wanting to hold back the tears that were threatening to swamp her. She closed her eyes and prayed that Jack would fall asleep quickly, like Jeff used to do. She could leave the room and cry until her tears dried up in privacy.

Of course, she should leave now. But her voice would betray her tears.

Jack looked at the back of Laena's head. He didn't understand why she had suddenly turned away. He couldn't seem to find his voice to tell her how incredible what had just happened had been. His muscles felt like jelly. He didn't think he could move. It felt as if every muscle in his body had climaxed simultaneously. His nervous system was overloaded. To be honest, his brain was mush and he couldn't make much sense of it all beyond mind-blowing.

One thing was true, though. He had never had *that* happen before. He was surprised his heart was still beating. He rolled to his side and lifted his hand to rest on Laena's upper arm.

Laena's body jerked at the light touch.

Ignoring the reaction, he scooted closer, and pressed his body against her. Jack could feel the mingling of his heat against hers. His lips lowered to her shoulder as his hand moved forward to cup her breast. He caressed her lightly, barely squeezing her breast once.

Suddenly she bolted away, jumping from the bed.

Jack looked at her naked back, not sure what was happening. He spoke her name softly, "Laena?"

When she didn't turn, he asked her quietly, "Come back to bed, Laena."

Laena stiffened. She barely held her tears at bay, so how could she go back, and lie down beside him and pretend she was all right? How could she act like his reaction didn't matter? She didn't hear anything over the roaring in her head. *These crazy-making thoughts were making her batty!*

A few seconds later, Jack touched her shoulder.

She jumped and looked over her shoulder. The look of surprise that filled his eyes moments later told her that he had seen the tears on her cheeks in the dim light from moon. She tried to twist away.

Jack grabbed her arms and held her firmly in front of him. "What is wrong, Laena? Why are you crying?"

Laena struggled to break free of his hold, but he was too strong, and too determined. She finally peeked into his face. What she saw there made her stare, and then really look intently, but she didn't see any repulsion, or rejection. She sniffled and then swallowed, hoping she could speak without screwing it up and making a fool of herself. "Did what I just did, no…just do… I mean…were you disgusted by what I…how I touched you?" Laena forced out the words, feeling like her heart stopped beating while she waited his answer.

He didn't answer right away, and then he shook his head slowly. His hands lifted to cup the sides of her face. "My God, Laena! I've never, ever experienced anything that intense before in my life. I was surprised but, sweetheart, disgusted doesn't have any place between us. Your touch is making me crazy. My body is going to go on strike, I think, to get some rest!" He kissed her lips lightly, gently.

"Come back to bed, my sweet, where it is warm." Jack took her hand and helped her into bed. He moved around and got in on the other side. She lay on her side, watching him. Jack turned and faced her. "I think we need to discuss this once. I loved my wife, Laena. Celia was a kind woman and a good wife. I missed her terribly after she was gone, and I might not have survived if not for my boys, the family and my work. But she never, ever made me feel the way you do. I'm telling you this so we only have the two of us in this bed."

Laena saw the truth in his eyes. The man had an honest face, which is probably why he was so well liked. She nodded. "I thought I loved Jeff. He was the first man I'd ever been with. I never questioned the way we made love. The magazines all said once a week or month even, was normal for most married people. Then one day I read this book, and thought I would try something with him." She stopped abruptly, as memories washed over her.

Jack reached over and touched her arm, pulling her back to the present. "Go on, honey."

"He acted like I was something disgusting that he'd stepped in and couldn't wait to scrape me off his shoe! After that, he rarely touched me, always having an excuse. Once we moved here, we were strangers living in the same house. I reminded him about his promise to start a family once he was settled—" She stopped and met Jack's eyes. "Anyway, you know the rest."

Silence followed her confession. She felt nervous as she waited for Jack to say something.

Finally, he lifted his hand from her arm and caressed the side of her face. "Laena, Jeff Hunt is an asshole and a fool. I can't begin to tell you how happy I am that he is such a stupid jerk. If he weren't, I wouldn't be here with you."

Several seconds passed as his words penetrated her conscious thoughts. Laena felt a warm flame deep inside her body flare to life as the phrases and sentences finally made sense. She didn't know what would happen between them, but suddenly the future wasn't worrying her. Today was what was important. She moved forward and kissed him softly.

Jack shifted in bed and cradled her head on his chest.

As she lay there, she knew that only time would completely heal her wounds from the past. Jeff's hurtful words and actions would fade now because Jack's assurance helped her realize that she was okay. For now it wasn't clear whether that she wouldn't relapse once in a while, feeling guilt overwhelm her again. Laena knew for sure that she'd do better. And with each time she fought back the demons in her past, she'd feel stronger.

In less time than it took for a deep breath, she was asleep in his arms.

Chapter Twelve

Laena sat at her wheel, watching the pot she'd started whirl aimlessly around and around. Her thoughts were too chaotic to really focus, but she had not been much use to Ruth in the house. Finally, Ruth told her to go out to the workroom and find something to do. So, for the last hour, she had been going from one thing to another, unable to focus long enough to do much of anything.

The problem was Jack. No more denying it. He was inside her head, and he was making her emotions into a quagmire of confusion. She had thought she could handle an affair. After all, she was a modern woman, right? She couldn't help but blush when she saw Ruth sometimes. All of her arguments that she was being silly still didn't stop the guilt. She felt like she was a teen having sex under her parents' roof. But, good lord, she had rationalized to herself, Jack was forty-eight and she was thirty-six. They weren't kids any longer. He had grown sons, so they should be able to live their lives any way they wanted.

Today Jack had left shortly after breakfast. He had been considerate by making breakfast first. He explained that he had some errands that couldn't be put off, but he would be home in time for dinner. He pecked his mother's cheek, took a last sip of coffee, and then grabbed Laena's hand. He smiled at his mother. "Laena will be right back, Mother. I need her to walk to the car with me."

Outside, though, he leaned against the door and pulled her close against him.

Nestled between his widespread thighs, she couldn't resist wiggling her hips, which earned a light, teasing slap to her fanny.

He bent his head and nearly kissed her socks off.

She was breathless when he finally set her away from him. She raised one hand and fanned her flushed cheeks, which caused Jack to smile knowingly and grin.

She wandered back into the house after watching the car disappear down the road.

In the kitchen, Ruth was busy at the sink. Turning, she smiled at her.

Laena was surprised when the older woman turned away from her quickly. She wondered if perhaps Ruth had an idea that only one of the beds was being used each night, even though Laena deliberately took the sheets off both.

The first morning when Jack had seen her running back to his room and removing those sheets as well, he had stopped her. "What are you doing? I watched as you put these clean on here yesterday. And unless we have poltergeist, no one has slept on this bed."

"If you were watching me, why didn't you help?" she answered quickly, trying to put off his real question. She knew that Jack would shake his head and laugh at her once he knew the truth. It was silly, but for some strange reason she thought it necessary to maintain the illusion they were not sleeping together. Nonsensical, she was sure, but it seemed the right thing to do in Ruth's house.

"Because it too much fun watching you bounce and jiggle while you were doing it."

Frustrated at feeling like she lived a lie under her dearest friend's roof, she had thrown the sheets towards

Jack. But he had been much too quick and a moment later, they fell to the floor on top of the other sheets. In almost the blink of an eye, their heated kisses led the way to making love on the floor. She had been surprised when he pulled a condom from his pocket.

She touched the foil packet before he could tear it, meeting his gaze.

Jack shrugged. "I know I should have thought of this sooner, but I admit when I'm with you, my brain isn't getting anywhere near enough blood for logical processes."

"No, it's my responsibility as well. I was tested —"

"Shh. It's okay, and from now on we'll be good, responsible adults."

She soon noticed that he had bought a large box for each bedroom and even one for the studio. Knowing he stashed one in his pocket for "just in case" scenarios like this helped her feel sexy and delightfully naughty.

Hearing the dishes clinking together drew Laena's attention back to the present and Ruth's kitchen. "Sorry! I was thinking about a new pot design," she added the small lie quickly.

Ruth looked back at her dishes quickly, seeing the flushed look on the younger woman's face. Perhaps she should feel guilty, but she did not. Ruth felt quite gleeful in fact. She was more than delighted with the way things were continuing.

She followed them to the living room. From behind the curtains, she had watched, enjoying the passionate scene and telling herself the whole time that her action was not spying. After all, it was *her* house! She could stand in any room, or look out any damned window she wanted!

The kiss she'd witnessed had answered any questions she'd had about her son and her companion.

And now, she tried hard not to reveal her joy to Laena. As they began the usual round of daily household chores, Ruth put up with her inattention for as long as she could stand it, and then shooed her to the studio.

* * * * *

Laena turned the music on before she started on the wheel, hoping it would help her focus. She still couldn't seem to get her act together, though, as she stared at the lopsided pot on her wheel. It looked so sad, she almost laughed. Her hair had fallen and she thoughtlessly used her clay-covered fingers to push it back. Disgusted with herself, she finally turned off the wheel and got up. Stretching from side-to-side, and then bending backwards, she tried to work some of the kinks and tightness out.

"Hello, Laena."

Laena gasped, spinning to see Jeff standing just inside the closed door of the studio. Before she could say anything, she saw his gaze travel down her body slowly, and then back up. She wore jean shorts and a midriff-length white cotton T-shirt. She flushed, seeing his gaze linger on her unbound breasts. She reached for the clay pot she had been working on, and walked over to her long bench. She slammed the clay onto the table, hitting it forcefully with her fist.

"What brings you out this way, Jeff? Shouldn't you be in the office, healing the sick, fooling around with your nurses?" Laena felt bad after she made the last comment. She should have kept her mouth shut, because he would probably assume she was jealous. And the truth was that he couldn't be farther from the truth. The testiness and rancor she felt came from the fact that he'd let it go on for so long, not telling her. Just like a cuckolded husband of the past, she felt the fool. But she would not give him the satisfaction and didn't look up.

Jeff began walking towards the bench. He stood back several feet, though, once he saw the small bits of clay go flying past him. "Why are you still here, Laena? You said you were moving back home." Jeff glared, angry at finding out she had not left as he had thought.

"This is now my home, Jeff. Ruth and I are getting along quite well," Laena told him tersely, not looking up as she spoke.

"How much?" Jeff gritted his teeth. There was no way that he would let her get the better of him, damn it all! Besides, Arlene had bit off his head several times since the night of the dinner. Hell! Even the baby had been acting up since that night. He was sure he could buy Laena out of town. Still feeling prideful at how little he'd let her get in the divorce, he was positive she hurt for money.

Finding the kiln and the pottery wheel here didn't make him feel much better. With these, she had a good chance to establish herself and become as popular an artisan as she'd been when he'd first met her. Now she was older which undoubtedly would have improved her talent—hell! He had kept her from starting up in a major way when they moved here, telling her she needed to be free to get them settled. Then he'd made sure to sell her kiln as soon as she moved out with their separation. His plan had been to make sure she had no way to stay in town and be forced to move away. Arlene had certainly expressed her desire to have his ex-wife leave town.

Finally, Laena looked up from the clay she pounded. She shook her head. "How much what, Jeff? What are you talking about?"

"Damn it! Laena, you are so ridiculously naïve sometimes. I'll pay you to move out of town. Now, how much do you want?"

"Look, Jeff." Laena couldn't stop the laugh that bubbled up from inside. This was better than any of the confrontations she'd had with him in her head. "We haven't seen each other in the almost two years since we divorced except that one time. There is very little chance we will meet very often. And hey, if I see you or Arlene coming down the street, I'll cross the street to get out of your way. That should take care of any concerns you have."

Jeff stepped forward and pounded his fist on the table. "No! Just knowing you are still in town is upsetting Arlene."

"And that is supposed to affect me? You want me to leave town because the woman you had an extramarital affair with doesn't want to see me? One of you is insane." Laena splattered some water onto her clay, and folded it over just once and then smashed it with her fist. A multitude of little bits of clay flew outward, in several directions.

"Laena, there is no reason for you to stay. You don't have any family here. I know you don't have any friends here either. I'll pay to move you and give you enough to buy a house. Hell, I'll even throw in enough to support you for a year until you get back on your feet. I think that is more than generous."

Laena snorted in disbelief. "You screw me during the divorce and leave me with little more than the clothes on my back. And now you say money is no object to get rid of me. I find it hard to believe this is all because Arlene is upset."

Laena bent her head once again and concentrated on pounding the clay flat, smiling as the clay flew wildly around the table.

Suddenly, Jeff reached across the table and grabbed her wrist. He twisted her arm.

She cried out softly.

Jeff didn't release her though, twisting a little further. "Now I get it! You're fucking Jack Spencer, aren't you, Laena? That's why you don't want to leave, isn't it? If you think something will come of it, you are fooling yourself. He may fuck you for a good time, and he always did like chicks with big tits. But he rides way too high on the social and political ladder for you. Once he decides what he wants to do next career-wise, he'll drop you so fast your head will spin. No way would he ever let you set foot into his world."

"Let go of her arm, Jeff."

Jeff turned, seeing Jack standing inside the studio. He released Laena's arm. "Hello, Jack. I didn't realize you were home."

Jack strolled slowly into the room. He was dressed in washed-out jeans and a white T-shirt.

Laena couldn't help but notice that even though Jack was seven years older than Jeff, he was much more physically fit, and he actually gave off a more youthful appearance. She met Jack's gaze and smiled slowly. Jeff's shock and what she was sure was a growing fear, felt good, and made her feel a little guilty.

Jack came around the bench and reached out to turn Laena's face towards him. He slowly lowered his mouth to hers, kissing her deeply. As he pulled away, he rubbed his thumb across her lower lip. "Looks like you've had an unsuccessful day at the wheel, my sweet."

Laena smiled and shrugged. She watched as Jack turned to slowly look at Jeff. "What brings you out here today? I didn't think you made house calls any more."

"I came to see Laena about something. Look, we'll talk later about this. I need to get back to the office." He took a step towards the door when Jack's voice stopped him.

"You're wrong about a lot of things, Jeff. But foremost is that you won't be coming back out here unless you are invited. Laena is staying here, for as long as she chooses. And lastly, I would be proud to introduce her to the former President, my friend, should the opportunity present itself. Now, goodbye, before I forget our families are friends."

The loud slam of the door, followed by a slight rattling marked Jeff's departure. Laena turned to look at Jack. "You are back early."

Jack grinned and pulled her close.

Laena shrieked, trying to keep her clay-covered hands from his pristine shirt.

But it was obvious that he didn't care as he kissed her again. "I missed you."

Laena felt the warmth deep inside her body flare to life. The more time she spent with Jack, the more she kept having these feelings. Wild, crazy and foreign to her, but definitely they were feelings she intended on exploring for as long as she could. She looked up into his smiling eyes. "I missed you, too. Ruth chased me outside because she kept tripping over me. I can't seem to focus on anything."

Jack's hands cupped her ass and pulled her closer.

She gasped. "Oh!"

He gently moved against her, letting her feel his erection against her belly. Jack lowered his head to kiss the side of her neck. "I'm having the workmen come back out and make a few additions to the studio tomorrow."

Laena leaned away, looking confused. "Why?"

Jack smiled. "For one thing, we need a shower out here. I thought a closet, to keep an extra change of clothes in, and maybe a small bedroom also."

Laena grinned, shaking her head. "With a twin-size bed?"

"I was thinking more along the lines of a full-size bed. The perfect size for cuddling."

Laena laughed and gave up trying to keep Jack clean. She wrapped her clay-covered hands and arms around him. "If you do that, next thing we'll be doing in here is throwing pots in the nude."

Jack grinned. "I like that idea. Your hands on the pot and my hands on your honey pot." He spun her around and walked her over to the sofa. Two seconds later, she was on her back with her shirt shoved up under her arms, and her shorts pulled down. Less than one second after that, Jack's jeans dropped and he tore open a foil packet.

"Can I help?" she asked him, barely above a whisper.

Jack shook his head. "Not this time, sweetheart, or things will be over before they get started!" About ten seconds later he was on top of her and sliding into her body.

"Oh, God!" he cried out.

"Is something wrong, Jack?" Laena asked him quickly.

Jack shook his head, taking a deep breath. "It's just that when I feel you...around me —" His voice broke off abruptly. He curled his hands around her hips, and set a rhythm that was slow and languorous.

Laena clawed at his back, trying to urge him to go faster. "I know, Jack. When you are inside me, I feel —"

Stopping abruptly, she'd almost said "complete". Thank God, she hadn't been so lost in her passion that she'd spoken without thinking. Sometimes saying too much to a man was the absolute worst thing to do...

Jack smiled and lowered his mouth to suck her nipple. "Jeff was right about one thing. You are beautiful and have the most gorgeous breasts."

Laena froze for a second. "Your type?"

Jack lifted his mouth from her breast. "I have no type, Laena. My sons' mother and now you happen to be the only two women I've had more than a third date with. Celia and I were high-school sweethearts. Before the election, I had a few first dates, engineered by well-meaning friends, one of whom became our commander-in-chief."

Laena chuckled. "And did he try and fix you up once he was the commander?"

"The First Lady tried once." Jack continued his steady movement in and out. "Then Tom cut her off at the pass the second time. He told her that if I got busy with a woman, he'd have less time for her. It worked."

Laena responded to his slow thrusts by rotating her hips and tightening her muscles. "Since then?"

"Only you, darling. And like I said, you have scrumptious boobs. They are luscious, natural and kind of Mother Earth."

"Eww!"

"No! I mean that in the nicest way. You are warm, loving and soft, both inside and out. It's hard to describe, sweetheart."

Laena tightened her muscles. "I'll stop talking and let you concentrate on this 'hard'. I think I've distracted you."

"You naughty—" He could only stand a few moments of her actions. He shifted to ease his hand between their bodies. His fingers found her clit and worked it rhythmically.

Laena lost control completely. Her climactic contractions pulled and sucked on his cock.

Jack stopped fighting the need and he came a few moments later.

Laena wrapped her arms around him, holding him close when he tried to pull away. She begged him to just wait, for a few moments.

Jack lifted his head to meet her eyes. He smiled slowly.

She saw him open his mouth to tell her—

"Jack! Telephone call!"

Laena heard him mutter "damn" as they heard Ruth's voice over the intercom installed between the house and studio.

A moment later, he slid off her body. He righted his own clothing and then stepped over to where he had tossed her jean shorts a few minutes earlier. He handed her the shorts and said he had to take the call.

Laena watched him sprint the distance to the house as she refastened her pants. She shook her head to clear her thoughts. All he had to do was touch her, and she became someone more than she had ever been before. She liked the feelings, but she was afraid she was falling in love with him. Of course, that assumed that she wasn't already head over heels for him.

Chapter Thirteen

Laena turned as Jack called her name. She pushed her hair back off her face, knowing they would have to be leaving soon. She set the timer on her kiln, and then started up to the house. She didn't see him on the back porch, and figured he had gone inside to finish getting everything together for them to leave.

She walked up the back stairs and straight to the bathroom. She dropped her clothes as she went, stepping straight into the shower. She let the shower course down over her body. She was surprised at how hot it was for July. Where had the months gone? The last four months with Jack had been her slice of heaven.

She washed her hair and then put on conditioner. She grabbed her razor and shaved her legs and underarms quickly. She ran her fingers across her smooth mound, smiling to herself as she remembered their shared shaving party last night. She hoped they hadn't been so loud that they had awakened Ruth. Of course, Ruth was too much of a lady to ever say anything.

Turning off the water, she stepped out of the shower. Combing her hair and quickly braiding it, Laena secured it with a small band. She walked into the bedroom, idly looking through her clothes for what to wear.

Walking into the bedroom, Jack found Laena naked, damp and obviously undecided on what to wear. He grinned and walked up behind her. Jack found it impossible not slide his hands around her waist, pleased that she had put on a little weight. It looked good on her, rounding her belly and hips a bit. He moved his hands upwards and cupped her breasts. He found her nipples were already taut and eager for his touch. He had noticed that her breasts had gotten a little bigger as well, and he certainly wasn't going to complain about that. Playing with her breasts had become his most favorite hobby.

Laena sighed and leaned back against him. She tilted her head as she felt his lips nibbling at her neck.

"God! I wish we could stay home and just fool around for a while," Jack whispered into her ear.

Laena's hands lifted to cover his as they cupped her breasts. "We would have more time for fooling around if you hadn't decided to supervise all the additions going on around here. Not to mention having the workmen hanging about makes the studio out of bounds for awhile."

Jack kissed his way up her neck. "Guilty as charged. But just think how much fun we'll be having out there once all this is done. With the phone line added, calls can be transferred, or the answering machine turned on or off from the house and the studio."

"What will your sisters think though when they find out about the deck you've added to the house and the hot tub?"

Jack turned her in his arms and hugged her close. "I've got an explanation for that—hydrotherapy for mother." Laena's laugh made him smile. He released her just enough for him to lean back and see her clearly. "Plus, I got Frank to back me up on that one. I'm more concerned about what they will think about the new pool."

"Pool! Are you crazy, Jack?" Laena cried out, shaking her finger admonishingly.

Jack stepped back hurriedly, after sneaking in a quick squeeze to her right ass cheek. "Not yet, and you'd better hurry up and get dressed. Besides, the pool was Mom's idea."

"What should I wear, Jack? My jeans are too tight lately. I'm going to have to go on a diet."

Jack grinned and chuckled. He moved in close behind her once again, reaching out to cup her breasts from below and bounce them gently in his hands. "Not on my account, darlin'. I like my toys big and soft."

That earned him an elbow in his stomach. She reached in and pulled out a summer-weight long cotton dress, which was composed mostly of lace, with a flesh-colored lining. Moving away from Jack and over to the dresser bureau, she started looking through the drawer for a bra and panties. She slipped the bra on and then looked up and saw that Jack was lying on the bed and watching her through the mirror.

He grinned seeing how small the bra had gotten. The way her breasts mounded above and spilled over the sides and out the bottom made him smile.

She usually didn't wear any around the house, and other than weekly trips to the grocery store, they hadn't been going many places in public.

Laena turned to frown at Jack. "I can't wear this. It is too tight, damn it."

Jack shrugged. "We'll make a trip to the city next week for some new clothes. I like the new rounded you."

Laena shook her head. She removed the bra and tried the panties. They were too tight as well. "I will have to get a scale. I hadn't realized I had gained this much weight. Ruth is too good of a cook. I'll have to start exercising."

She slipped the dress on over her head and sat on the bed for Jack to fasten the small button at her back.

"Maybe I should start taking you out jogging with me in the mornings."

"I don't do my best that early in the day, Jack," Laena reminded him as she adjusted the neckline that hinted at her cleavage.

Jack laughed softly and kissed the tender skin just above the button at the base of her neck. "Well, we could work on a schedule to have sex three times a day. I think I heard that burns off two hundred calories. When the guys go for their afternoon break, I'll tell them I'll be back in twenty. Ow!"

Laena's elbow connected quite well with his stomach. "I'm sure it will all balance out now that I'm aware of it. I'll just watch what I eat. Before you came back, I never had this problem, I'll have you know." She stood and walked back to the dresser.

"So, now you want to blame me, huh? I'm a bad influence?" Jack laughed as he stood. "Grab your shoes, Laena. We need to get a move on, or we'll be late."

* * * * *

Jack parked near his siblings' cars. He carried the picnic basket and their lightweight chairs. Jack pointed to a large gathering around three picnic tables.

Laena had the small cooler and blankets they had added. A moment later, Chris and John, Patrick's sons, ran over and eagerly relieved Laena of her burdens. She laughed though as Jack cleared his throat and looked pointedly at the chairs and basket that he was carrying.

Both boys blushed and reached out to take his items as well.

Jack took Laena's hand as they walked more slowly, following the boys. He squeezed her hand. "Don't worry so, honey. My sisters will behave themselves, or else."

Laena shook her head and laughed. She started to reply, "Well—"

Michael walked over to them, smiling at Jack. He leaned over to kiss Laena's cheek. "We haven't seen you for so long, Jack, Pat wondered if you hadn't moved back to DC."

Laena flushed, but smiled at Michael.

Jack started to reply, when he heard David and Daniel calling. "I'll be right back," he muttered. "Laena, honey, just wait here. And you, Michael, behave yourself."

Michael grinned. "Jack forgets sometimes that I've actually grown up."

Laena shook her head. "He truly appreciates everything that you've accomplished, Michael. I've heard him talking to your mother about all of you."

"Hmm," Michael nodded his head. "I was a teenager when Jack married Celia, so I don't remember a whole lot of that time. I was tuned into my own angst against the world. I do know that I've never seen Jack act as he does when he's around you."

Laena stopped her leisurely, slow walk. "What do you mean? He doesn't talk a whole lot about the past, and Celia. I know he was happy, and he missed her terribly."

"Yeah, her death was tough on everyone. He would have pulled out of the campaign except she refused to let him do it. After she was gone, I know the boys missed their dad at times, but his job is what kept him sane until the worst of the grief went away."

"It's amazing that Daniel and David turned out so well-adjusted. Technically, you could say they lost both their parents, considering the high-stress job Jack was about to begin."

"True, Laena, but Jack was always here for big events, and we had huge phone bills. You'd have to ask the boys if they suffered."

"They don't appear to have. The time I've spent with them hasn't been much, but I like each of them."

"Me too," Michael chuckled. "I guess what I meant to say is that I don't ever remember seeing Jack act this blatantly possessiveness over a woman. He seemed like a monk at times, but the few women I saw him with were never treated the way he does you."

"Is that your way of saying something in particular? I know your sisters and the sisters-in-law don't like me. Are you adding your disapproval as well?" Laena started walking towards the others.

Michael reached out and stopped her.

She turned back, smiling.

"It's none of my business, Laena." Michael held onto her upper arm lightly. "And feel free to tell me to shut up, but I'm changing the subject. Have you put on weight? I'm only asking because I'm concerned. You've been through a lot of stress, and I doubt you've seen a doctor lately, either."

Laena blushed. "A lady doesn't like discussing her weight, Michael."

Michael grinned, but was undeterred. "Are you feeling all right?" He reached out and touched the dark circle beneath one eye. "Do you know how much weight you've put on?"

Laena shook her head. "I've been a little tired, Michael, but the weather is hot and I've spent a lot of time in the studio. Besides, I thought doctors only got concerned when people lost weight."

"Call me a worrier, but will you please come with me in a little bit to the office? Let me just take a quick blood sample to check your hemoglobin and a few things. Make an old man happy."

Laena laughed, shaking her head. "You are not old, Michael. But all right, just tell me when you are ready."

Ruth called her name, so Laena excused herself to Michael. She walked over to where Ruth was seated on a lounge chair, next to Frank Hunt. Since the dinner back in March, the two of them had become something of an item. They went to dinner at least once a week, but many times, he had come to the house and the four of them would eat and watch a movie or play cards.

"You look lovely, dear. Did you get finished in the studio?" Ruth smiled.

Laena nodded, accepting a folding chair from Frank. "Yes. Jack let me work as long as possible while he put the lunch together. I've got the timer set for the kiln. Hopefully, when we get home, it will have cooled off enough to be checked."

Frank smiled and took his seat on the other side of Ruth again. "What have you been working on?"

"Actually, it is a joint project." She smiled at Ruth. "Ruth has been getting some books from the library and reading up on different glazes. We are working on some pots together. Ruth works the clay sometimes, I throw them on the wheel, and then we discuss and plan the glazes together."

Ruth grinned at Frank, reaching over to take his hand. "I'm quite excited. We have a couple of stores that want to carry our pots, so this way we will be able to be more efficient."

Frank squeezed Ruth's hand. "May I be one of the first to see your newest accomplishments?"

Ruth blushed and turned to Laena. "Maybe this evening when you take me back home."

Laena nodded, seeing the excitement in her dearest friend's face. She was pretty sure Ruth was on her way to falling in love with Frank, if she wasn't already. She couldn't help but wonder what her dear friend's daughters thought of this relationship.

"Heads up!"

Laena looked up and caught the ball thrown her way. She smiled at John who had tossed her the ball. "I'm afraid I didn't dress to play today."

Chris frowned as he came up next to his brother. "Darn. Well, save me a place beside you at the table and I'll forgive you."

"Me too!" John added quickly.

Jack came up behind her and put his hands on her shoulders. "Sorry, guys, she only has two sides, and one is mine."

Both boys groaned, but then asked their uncle if he wanted to join the game.

He agreed and said he'd be back to claim his side at the table. Jack leaned down and kissed her mouth slowly, and very deliberately.

She could feel the heated flush moving up her neck and staining her cheeks.

He winked at her as he pulled away, and then jogged off to join the game. As she looked back from watching him cross the field, she found Ruth's gaze trained on her. After a few moments, Ruth grinned.

A few minutes passed and then Ruth and Frank went over to watch the game. She thought about joining them, but it was so much nicer here, in the shade. A moment later, she felt a light touch on her arm and looked up to see Michael standing beside her. She saw the questioning look in his eyes. Pushing away her reluctance, she nodded and followed him in the opposite direction of the game, to his office.

Once inside, Michael slipped on his white coat and became the perfect professional. He asked his questions straightforwardly. "When did you last see a gynecologist, Laena? I don't see in your records that you've been in our offices for quite some time."

Laena felt the heated blush steal up her neck and across her cheeks. She'd never felt comfortable when she visited the office, even before the divorce. Afterwards, she wouldn't risk running into Jeff or Arlene. She'd felt healthy. "It's been a couple of years. But I've been very healthy and no problems."

Michael looked up from his papers. "Method of birth control?"

Laena had to swallow hard to answer that one. "Condoms."

"Nothing else?"

Laena heard the surprise in his voice. As she answered she knew her blush darkened by at least ten degrees. "Um, no. I wasn't sexually active—" her voice faded. All of a sudden, she felt like a guilty teen.

"Number of sexual partners?"

Nothing could have prepared her for his next question. It almost knocked her off the table. She considered lying, but then figured he probably already knew. "You mean total, as in all that I've ever had?"

"Yes."

"Two," she told him softly.

Michael nodded, and quickly examined her heart and lungs. "Everything sounds good, Laena."

She was most surprised to find that she had gained almost fifteen pounds! And she was relieved when he drew a couple tubes of blood and then had her leave a specimen in the bathroom.

Michael told her she could leave after that, and he would follow her after he closed up the office.

Laena shrugged, assuming he'd run the tests or whatever he needed to do when the office reopened after the holiday. Quite honestly, that suited her fine because she didn't enjoy doctor visits, at least not to this office building. Slowly, she walked back to the city park.

Chapter Fourteen

The game had just ended when she reached the tables. The park seemed more crowded than when she had left, and she saw that many of the Spencer family was still involved in an impromptu softball game. Hoping to sit with Ruth, Laena stopped at the table where the food was being spread out by Jack's sisters and sisters-in-law. Gingerly she took a potato chip, popping it into her mouth.

In the months since Christmas, the heat from the female half of the family had seemed less intense. After the initial blowup over the studio, which occurred over the holiday after Jack's departure, there had been very few disruptive calls or conversations.

"Would you like something to drink? We have a little longer before we eat."

Laena turned and saw Jack's sister Cindy was standing on the other side of the table, looking at her. "Oh, hi, Cindy. Sure, that sounds good. How much longer will they be playing, you think?"

At that moment, Janet walked up carrying two glasses. "Lemonade or iced tea?" She offered Laena a choice.

"Thank you, Janet. Um, lemonade, please." She sat down on the picnic bench that had been pulled about two feet from the table.

"No problem, and the game won't be over until one of the 'Dads' admits he can't take another step. The 'Sons' are killing them out there."

Cindy laughed at her sister's accurate description. "Exactly, Jan. David was telling Sarah at the last inning that the only chance the 'poor Dads'—using his words—was if you were playing on the Dads' team."

Janet nodded. "It only makes sense they'd win. They've got six boys, aged fourteen to twenty, all of whom play sports, both during school and the summer."

"Then you have five middle-aged men, of whom the oldest looks like he's in the best shape—"

"Do you really think so, Cindy?" Janet questioned her sister, looking over towards the ball field.

Laena considered agreeing, but this friendly attitude still had her baffled.

"Oh, yeah! Uncle Jack is the hunkiest of the bunch, although it isn't the kind of thing I care to think about, personally."

Laena, Janet and Cindy turned to see Michael's sixteen-year-old daughter Mandy.

Mandy grinned. "Don't look so surprised! Now, Mom sent me looking for my Dad. Anyone see him?"

Laena nodded. "Yes, he's at the office."

Mandy turned to go, but glanced over her shoulder to add, "If you were playing Laena—"

"I know, I know. I'm guilty as charged, I guess." Laena threw up her hands and then waved as Mandy ran off.

Things were silent between the three women for nearly a minute.

Janet cleared her throat.

Cindy nodded, shifting on the bench opposite Laena. "Laena."

"Yes?"

"We owe you an apology," Cindy said, gesturing to her sister. "We didn't give you a chance when you moved in with Mother."

"It's okay," Laena offered quickly, sure this was hard for both women.

Janet sat beside her sister. "No, we really were pretty bitchy, and we stirred up the sisters-in-law to go along with us."

"Unfortunately for you that was fairly easy when they saw how pretty you are."

"Thank you, but I do understand how you must have felt. I was a stranger, living with your elderly mother," Laena said.

Cindy shrugged. "Yes, but you weren't really a stranger. You'd been married to Jeff, but we never bothered to get to know you."

"We better not let Mom hear us calling her elderly," Janet warned, glancing around nervously.

"She often has more energy than I do," Laena told Ruth's daughters.

"Me, too." Cindy bobbed her head vigorously. "That's partly what took me by surprise when she told us you were moving in. That plus the fact that it was Frank who was backing her up, not Michael."

Janet leaned forward, lowering her voice. "I've wondered many times if Mother was really ill, or did she concoct that just to have you move in?"

Cindy shrugged, shaking her head. "Who knows? What we do know is that Sally gathered us together after watching that psychologist on television."

"We were jealous...of you, Laena. It hurt that my Mom would choose to have a stranger in her home, rather than move in with *me*!" Janet's voice cracked at the end.

Cindy wrapped one arm around her sister. "What we finally understood was that even if Mother was perfectly healthy and still wanted you to live with her that we would choose the same thing. Who wouldn't want to remain in their own home, for as long as possible?"

Laena nodded. That is what she suspected Ruth's goal was from the beginning, and not the excuse the older woman had used — not wanting to impose on her children.

"Needless to say, Laena, we are sorry," Janet added again.

"It's okay. I understand how you felt. I would have done the same."

"You are too nice to let us off so easily," Cindy pointed out.

Laena shrugged.

"Hey, sisters! I need to steal Laena for a minute and talk to her," Michael interrupted.

Laena nodded and started to rise.

"You are supposed to bail out your brothers, Michael. The youngsters are creaming them." Janet laughed.

"I will," Michael replied, as he took hold of Laena's elbow. "I won't be long."

She started to speak as they walked towards the cars. "I hope you weren't smiling because of how much you want to charge me and not about the tests."

Michael glared at her as he came to a stop. Releasing her elbow, he immediately stepped away and leaned back against one of the families' cars. As he crossed his arms, a look of disgust appeared on his face.

Laena could feel her heart racing at Michael's behavior, asking him quickly, "What's wrong, Michael?"

A disgusted grunt preceded his reply. "I can't figure you out, Laena. I feel sorry for you, mostly because of the way Jeff treated you. But hell, that is no reason to seek out some weird, warped kind of revenge and use my brother to get it."

Laena reeled back a step at his vituperative glare. Michael's words felt like a slap across her face. "I don't know what you are talking about." She held her hands out placatingly. "I just wanted to know if you had done the tests or if you were going to wait until after the weekend."

"Does Jack know?" he asked her in a clipped fashion, almost growling out the words.

Laena shook her head, trying to clear her thoughts.

He snapped once more. "So, Jack doesn't know what a sap you've been playing him for, huh?"

"I don't know what—" Laena started to reply.

A deep voice interrupted her. "Does Jack know what, Michael?"

Michael flushed, suddenly feeling sorry for his brother, who didn't deserve to be hurt again. He was angriest at how Laena was so obviously deceiving Jack. Also, he couldn't believe she was in the dark. He scoffed as he recalled how naïve she'd acted about the weight gain. Oh, and yeah, she'd lied about the number of her sex partners, too!

When Michael didn't reply, Jack turned to look at Laena with a raised eyebrow.

Laena shook her head and shrugged.

"Don't lie to him, damn it!" Michael lashed out, feeling suddenly like a kid who needed to defend his brother, against all comers, no matter what. "I doubt my brother's powers of observation at the moment, as well."

"What are you talking about, Michael?" Laena held her hands up and out. "It was your idea to see me in the office and now you act like I am some kind of thief."

Jack frowned as he moved closer. "You saw Laena as a patient? When?"

Michael shrugged. "I thought she looked rundown, and well, even you must have noticed she'd gained some weight." He looked at his older brother accusingly.

Jack nodded, but replied, "So what? I think she looks beautiful, no matter what she weighs. And so long as she is healthy, who gives a damn about a few pounds." He smiled at Laena.

Michael snorted. "Fifteen pounds is not a few pounds. It may be spread around at the moment, but pretty soon everyone will know."

Laena glared at Michael, putting her fisted hands on her hips. "Know what? I don't know what the heck you are talking about."

Michael looked at his brother, who in turn gazed at Laena. "You're pregnant. I can't say how far yet—"

Laena gasped.

Jack's very definitive "no way!" drowned her out.

Michael looked at Laena again. "I noticed after you left that you put a question mark where it asked for your last period. Surely you had to wonder—" He paused, knowing he needed to keep his expression compassionate or at least not like was condemning her. He knew he was being completely unprofessional, but he was pissed off that Laena was stringing along his brother.

Laena turned to Jack. "No way?" She shook her head. "What do you mean, no way, Jack?" Before he could answer, she turned back towards Michael. "I have never had regular periods, and to be honest—" her gaze moved back to rest on Jack. "I didn't think about taking any precautions the first couple of times. I know it was wrong, and unsafe for reasons beyond pregnancy. If I had gotten pregnant, I would have been happy about it, Jack. I told you how I wanted a family, but Jeff wouldn't hear of it. But what do *you* mean by saying no way?"

Michael knew the answer to that question, and folded his arms across his chest waiting for his big brother to reply. He wasn't kept waiting too long.

Jack looked from Michael to Laena. "I had a vasectomy a few days before we discovered Celia's cancer. So, if you really are pregnant, it can't be mine." He stopped abruptly, crossing his arms over his chest.

Michael could see the pain on his brother's face. Damn! He hated reminding him of Celia and that painful time. Now it looked as if he'd fallen for a woman who was cheating on him, and they weren't even married yet!

Laena stared at Jack. "Nice of you to tell me that." She stopped abruptly. "Why have you been using condoms then? We never discussed birth control in detail, I know, but then you started using them. I probably should have still talked it over with you."

She stopped again, glaring at Jack and gulping back tears. "Since you knew you were shooting blanks, why would you bother? Did you think I had some kind of sexually transferable disease and I had not bothered to tell you? That says a lot about what you think of me, doesn't it?"

Jack shoved his fists into his pockets. "Damn it! I used the condoms because I wasn't ready to tell you about the vasectomy. Right from the beginning, you'd been honest about wanting a baby. I didn't want to blow my chances with you because I couldn't give you a baby. In the beginning, I didn't know where we were going, or anything. I mean maybe this thing between us was just something that would fade away."

Laena listened, nodding. Maybe it would have made a difference, if she'd known from the very beginning. But the attraction between them was so strong.

Nope!

There wasn't a doubt inside her. No way could she have turned away from him because he could not impregnate her. Now, it was moot anyway!

Tears welled up in her eyes as she looked at him. "You can think whatever you like, but I've not been with any other man but you, Jack, since long before my divorce was final. So, if Michael says I'm pregnant, and you say you had a vasectomy—" she paused as she gulped back her sobs. "Then I guess this must be some kind of a freaking miracle!"

Laena turned angrily from the men, and started walking down the road, away from the park. She tried wiping away the tears, but they came too fast. Instead, she walked faster, almost running once she was out of sight of the park.

Michael looked at his brother. "Um, Jack?"

Jack glared at his brother. "What, damn it?"

Michael wished to hell that he had not taken Laena to his office earlier. "Now that we've been talking about this and all, I remember that things were really hectic during that time."

"So?" Jack folded his arms across his chest. "God! This is insane, Michael! This up and down stuff drives me crazy."

"Well, you were my first vasectomy, after the special training course I had taken. And to be perfectly honest, well, um…I can't remember if you came back for your follow-up sperm count." Michael paused, seeing the look of disbelief on Jack's face.

Jack shook his head. "I remember having the damned thing done. I was still sore when Celia's doctor called, you know the specialist she'd seen. Then things went from hectic to crazy. Celia went downhill so quickly following her diagnosis." Jack paused. "I know all my attention was divided between her and the boys. She still insisted I go ahead with the campaign plans. Damn it all, Michael! I know I never had any sperm count test afterwards. I didn't see a doctor until we were in the White House and that isn't precisely something I felt right discussing *there*!"

Michael flushed and looked down at his feet. "This may seem awkward, but maybe we should go over to the office, and you could—"

Jack groaned, pounding his fist into his palm. "You want me to jerk off in your office while you wait! Holy crap! This holiday sure is going downhill fast!"

Michael tried not to, but he laughed in spite of his wishes.

Jack glared at his younger sibling as he spoke. "Well, brother, it appears that we screwed this up nicely, didn't we?"

Michael shrugged. "It's the only way to really be sure."

Jack shook his head. "No, I believe Laena." He fished in his pocket for his keys. "Why I doubted her… Tell Mother I'll see her later. I am going after Laena, and hopefully straighten this out between us." He stopped a few feet from his car and looked back at his brother. "You're sure? You ran the test twice?"

Michael nodded and watched as Jack climbed into his car and started after the mother of his unborn child. He started back towards the family but stopped when he saw his mother walking towards him. He smiled, but the curious and concerned look on her face told him that she had seen something and was determined to have an explanation.

"Michael, what's wrong?"

Michael walked the last few steps and put his arm around his mother's shoulders, turning them both towards the picnic area. "Technically, I'm not sure whose confidentiality I am bound to protect."

"Stop beating around the bush and *tell* me!"

"Jack is going to try and correct a mistake that he and I made. Let's just hope he is successful." Michael felt disgusted with his behavior, and what he'd said to Laena. But he'd been torn between loyalty to his big brother, who had always been there to rescue him, bail him out and even teach him the important stuff about women, and his oath. With chagrin, he reminded himself that was indeed why you didn't treat family members!

Now that he stopped to think about it, it had been stupid to even think about Laena having another relationship on the side. They lived in a small community, and everybody knew everyone else's business. The news about Laena and Jack, after their dinner together, had spread like wildfire. "I owe her an apology as well."

Ruth stopped abruptly, placing her hands on her hips and glaring at her son. "And if he isn't successful?"

Michael looked over to where the children were playing games. "Then you might not get to see your newest grandchild being born."

* * * * *

Laena hadn't gone too far when she heard a car coming up behind her on the quiet road. She wasn't at all surprised to hear Jack's voice. She didn't stop as he requested, but kept right on walking. She did stop when Jack pulled the car to a halt across the road, right in front of her, and thereby blocking traffic. She glared at Jack. "You'll get a ticket doing that."

Jack left the driver's door open and the engine running as he exited the car. He stopped in front of her. "Laena, I'm sorry for what I said back there. It was stupid and thoughtless. Also, after you left, Michael remembered he never performed the standard postoperative tests. Michael did the vasectomy and before it was time to check everything out again, Celia had been diagnosed with cancer and I never gave it a second thought. I assumed the procedure was successful."

A moment later, the whoop-whoop of a siren drew their attention. Jack turned, aggravated. He got even more pissed when he saw Howie Striker climbing from the squad car slowly, taking time to put on his hat, before walking towards them.

"Oh, hell," Jack muttered under his breath.

Laena turned to look as well. The grin was huge that split his face when he recognized first Jack, and then her.

The sheriff strolled up slowly. "Howdy there, Jack, ma'am. Did you have an accident of some kind, Jack?" He paused to push his hat back slightly off his forehead with his index finger. Next he hooked his thumbs into his belt loops, casually looking from Jack to Laena. "That certainly is a weird position to get your car into. Did the other vehicle hit you and run off?" Howie rocked forward and then back on his heels once, and then twice. "Were you a passenger, ma'am, or a witness?"

Jack grimaced. "No, Howie. Everything is fine and I'll move it in just a second."

Laena answered a split second later. "It was aliens. The bright light of their spaceship turned his car around."

Howie was a good and observant sheriff, as well as having been married nearly twenty years. He noticed the tear streaks down Laena's face, which hasty rubbing could not entirely obliterate. Doubtful that anything requiring legal intervention was going on, this was most likely little more than a little lover's spat. As sheriff, he usually got an earful of the latest gossip from his deputies. Considering what he had observed at Christmas, plus some other interesting tales regarding these two, this should prove entertaining, if nothing else.

"Is this man bothering you, ma'am?" he questioned, shooting a suspicious glance towards Jack.

Laena shot a look at Jack before she replied.

If nothing else, the look on the young woman's face told him they'd had a fight. He'd seen that same look on his wife's face plenty of times—right before she said something to make him feel more uncomfortable than he already did.

"Why, yes, sheriff. I was just walking along, minding my own business, when he pulled in front of me and cut off my path."

Howie nodded and pulled his hands from his pockets. He rocked on his heels a bit. "Well, now, this being the Fourth and all, we sure don't need anything disturbing the peace of our little community, now do we?"

Laena couldn't contain her gasp of laughter, which earned her a glare from Jack.

Howie removed his hat and scratched the top of his head. "Maybe I should arrest him?"

"What the hell for?" Jack almost spit at Howie.

Howie shrugged. "How about for possible future disturbance of peace?"

Laena laughed again. "If you arrest me as well, I'll make sure my one phone call is to the local paper. I'm sure they'd like to get a picture of a former high-ranking US official sitting in the local pokey."

Jack glared at Laena. "You, shut up!" He turned to frown at Howie. "You! Give me two minutes, and I'll move the car. You owe me that much for the time I covered for you with Bernadette."

Laena noticed the flush rapidly moving up the sheriff's neck.

"All right, Jack," Howie replied quickly. "Two minutes, and don't you ever bring that up again!" He turned towards his car, but stopped to look back a second later. He pointed at Laena. "And please, don't be joking about that alien stuff. I've got enough headaches." He got into his car, squealing the tires as he moved around Jack's car, and down the road, but not out of sight.

She saw Jack close his eyes for a moment. No doubt, he was getting ready to apologize and plead for her forgiveness. Without saying anything, she crossed her arms, waiting. As she continued standing there, idly tapping one foot, Jack looked at her a few moments longer. She could almost feel the emotions coming from him in waves.

"Before I met you, unprotected sex was never an issue." Jack flushed, looking embarrassed. "And when I'm with you, I don't think very efficiently. At least in the beginning it was that way, and then…" he paused, reaching up to rub at his temple on the left side. "I do know that after I stashed the condoms everywhere, I should have told you that I didn't need them, because of the vasectomy. I knew I was healthy and I had no doubt you were. I guess I was as reticent as you to discuss it.

"If one of boys acted like I have…well, thank God, they don't. I really do think I was more than half afraid you would decide you could do better than an old guy like me, who came with baggage." He paused, thinking. "There were a few times I guess…well, I should have brought up the subject. I know a few times I nearly asked if you were on the pill."

After running his hands through his hair, he pushed them into the back pockets of his jeans. "I've been too busy to keep up on the modern-day woman, sex and cities and all, but from what I'd heard a lot of women take the pill all the time, or get a long-lasting shot. The only other woman I'd shared any kind of safe-sex talk was with Celia, after we'd been married. She brought it up—the vasectomy as birth control."

Laena had to acknowledge the truth of his words. "It isn't your entire fault, Jack. And maybe, subconsciously, this is what I wanted. Otherwise, I would have been doing something to prevent it, or at least I would have chosen a backup method like Michael mentioned." She looked at Jack, holding his gaze for a moment. She walked around him and climbed into the car, sliding across the driver's seat.

Jack followed her quickly, slamming the door shut behind him. He put the car into gear and started back to the park. He stopped out of sight though, so no one in his family could see the car. After a few seconds, he turned on the seat, propping his right arm along the back of the seat.

Laena turned and looked at Jack. She wasn't sure what she expected to see in his eyes, but she hurriedly looked away. She knew she should face this head-on and deal with it, but it was all so new!

Looking down, her gaze seemed to settle on her tummy. For the first time, she noticed that instead of her arms being folded or just resting at her sides, both of her arms curved inwards and her hands protected her slightly rounded belly. Instinctively, she was already acting like a mother. Being a mother was something she had begun to doubt occurring in her life, unless a miracle happened. Slowly she realized that a miracle had happened. She'd met Jack! The baby was her second miracle.

"You wanted me to get you pregnant?" Jack's voice cracked as he repeated what had been echoing in his brain since she had said it a few minutes earlier. Damn! He could interpret her words several ways. But foremost was the overwhelming feeling of warmth as he considered that her desire to be pregnant could mean she was in love with him, and wanted to be bound to him in an undeniable and unbreakable bond. He was hesitant, though, to acknowledge how good this made him feel.

Laena looked at Jack and then away, back out the front window.

He heard her take a deep breath, and he wondered what she thought right now.

"Maybe I was jealous of Arlene," she murmured softly, continuing to stare out the glass.

A shock of pain went through him at her words. He didn't like the idea that she might have gotten pregnant out of jealousy over her ex-husband's new wife. Damn! Jack sure as hell didn't like the idea that she might have been pretending he was Jeff all along, just to get pregnant.

Laena spoke softly, staring off into the distance. "Arlene has everything that should have been mine."

Jack felt as if Laena's words were sharp knives, cutting into his flesh without any regard. He hadn't realized how intense his feelings for Laena were, until now. He had been happy just letting things drift along. Sure, it was a stupid thing to do, but he had been happy not dealing with questions about the future. Reaching over, he lightly touched her hair. Words were piling up inside of him, needing to be spoken.

"Hey!"

Jack and Laena turned and saw Daniel standing at the hood of the car, watching them. "Come on, you two. You are missing all the fun."

Daniel came around to Laena's side and pulled open her door. She climbed out, smiling at the young man. He offered her his arm and started walking her back to where the family was gathered.

Jack followed more slowly, pondering whether he should have demanded Laena stay and they talk it out now. He knew he was caught up in jealousy over Laena's words. He didn't like the idea that she wanted what Arlene had. That would mean she was still in love with her ex-husband.

He stopped a short distance from the family. Sitting at a deserted picnic table, he watched his family going about their holiday.

Children were running all over the place. David and his girlfriend had been glued together since her family had dropped her off about an hour after he'd arrived. It surprised him that he had not gotten to know this girl that would most likely become his daughter-in-law before too much longer.

Damn! He'd hoped he had ten more years before either of his sons would be considering a wife and children. The way life was going, he had a good chance to be a grandfather before he turned fifty. Watching the way the two kids were hanging on each other, they might end up presenting him with a grandchild before there was time for a wedding.

His thoughts and emotions weren't making much sense at the moment. Logically, he should be more concerned about learning that he was about to be a new dad at the age of forty-eight...wait. He'd be forty-nine before they got here. He had been so damned sure that possibility didn't exist. The only babies in his life would be grandchildren, and he had been very happy with that plan. He wasn't sure that he wanted to start all over. He could very easily remember how difficult life had been when the twins had been young. Sleepless nights were fine for a young man of twenty-eight, but, hell, he had nearly reached the point that when he missed sleep it showed! And he felt the lack for days.

Still, Laena had desperately wanted to have a baby. In the beginning, a part of his brain had told him to keep quiet about the vasectomy. While he wasn't sure what would happen, he sure as hell had known that he didn't want to blow any chance he might have. Many times he heard it from his sisters say that when a woman reached a certain age and she wanted children, any man that didn't would not get past her front door. And God knew that he had wanted to get way past the entryway!

"Penny for your thoughts?"

Jack turned in surprise to see his mother had managed to approach him, and he had been unaware of her presence until she spoke. "Inflation, Mom. They must be worth at least a quarter."

Ruth laughed and smiled at her eldest. He had always been the steadiest of all her children. She had never had to worry about Jack. Even as a teen, he had been levelheaded. But right now, it appeared her levelheaded, high-powered son had been knocked for a loop by fate. She considered pretending ignorance, but decided honesty was best. "I spoke with Michael, Jack."

Jack glanced over towards his brother, glaring. "Does patient confidentiality mean nothing these days?"

Ruth laughed, then reached over and patted her son's arm. "Don't blame Michael. You know he could never keep a secret from me. Whenever you kids were hiding something, it was always Michael who would cave under his mother's interrogation."

Jack laughed. "Yeah, though I'm not sure if it was Michael who couldn't keep a secret, or whether you missed your calling and should have been working for the government."

Ruth laughed, nodding. "Either way, I hope you worked it out with Laena. I'd enjoy having a baby in the house."

A startled look crossed his face.

Ruth grinned up at her tall son. "I love children, Jack. And I know Laena does, too. I think it's wonderful, even if it is a surprise."

"Michael should have his license revoked." Jack half jested.

"What's done is done, Jack. Forget about that and worry about making a home for your child. One good thing is you won't lack for babysitters." Ruth turned to look across to where Laena was playing with his nieces and nephews. "Laena is very popular with all my grandchildren." Ruth pointed to where Laena was with Jenny and Melissa, both fifteen, chatting as if she were their peer. "At their age, all they want to do is rebel against their parents, especially mothers, for the girls anyway. But they listen to Laena. She's more hip…if that's the right word."

Ruth paused, watching as her son let his gaze move to Laena, and down her body. She could just imagine what he must be thinking. "I never would have guessed that she was pregnant yet. But then I guess that is where Michael's trained eye comes in. We'll need to find a good obstetrician." She paused, waiting for Jack to turn towards her once more and give her his full attention. She didn't have to wait more than a few seconds. She smiled before continuing. "After all, she certainly can't see Jeff for her prenatal care."

Ruth stopped to let that thought sink into what she had started to think was her son's *thick* head.

* * * * *

Embarrassed, Jack realized he had stared at Laena's nearly flat stomach for more than a minute. He tried to imagine her belly swollen with child. He was well acquainted with pregnant women, what with his sisters and sisters-in-law. But this was something new and unusual. It felt different from when he had learned Celia was pregnant, followed by the news that it was twins. Just the idea of watching as Laena progressed through pregnancy appealed to him.

He had listened to his brothers and friends over the years all complaining about their wives' bodies as they got bigger. He wasn't turned off in the least by the thought of her body slowly changing. If anything, it excited him to imagine the changes her body would soon begin to experience over the next months. He wasn't ready to reveal his insecurities though.

Quickly Jack decided to change the subject. "I'll probably need to talk to my sisters and get them to come around and warm up to Laena."

Ruth shook her head. "Surprisingly, you won't have too. I had a talk with Cindy and she told me about a chat she had with Laena. She reassured me that Janet and your sisters-in-laws are in agreement. I will be arranging a baby shower soon. We just need to decide whether to include the men or not."

Coming to his feet, he reached down and helped his mother to her feet. "Come on, Mother. Let's rejoin the festivities. We can talk about this later."

Chapter Fifteen

Laena lay alone in her bed that night. Jack had seemed distant on the drive home, and he had made no effort to touch or kiss her since learning of her pregnancy. She didn't know what to think. A good chance existed that he would reject her soon. After all, he'd had a vasectomy because he didn't want more children. And that decision had been made more than nine or ten years earlier. Certainly, he was even surer of the possibility now. Fear bubbled inside her over the future.

After an hour of tossing and turning in her bed, she crept from the house and made her way to the studio. She turned on only one light and began working the clay. Soon, she was seated at the wheel, wearing one of Jack's white T-shirts that had been in her drawer. With the clay in her hands, she felt much calmer. She would need to make some decisions, and soon. Watching the pot begin to take shape, she started to cry. Her life had finally begun straightening out and now everything seemed bent on going haywire again.

Laena guessed she would have to leave here. This was Jack's home, after all, not hers. She didn't expect Ruth to choose her over her son. She would never let it come down to that. Soon she would have to start looking for somewhere to live. Ignoring the soreness in her back, Laena worked until dawn, trying to concentrate on the clay and not on her chaotic and disorganized thoughts. Tears coursed down her cheeks at irregular intervals, and

Laena used her clay-covered fingers to wipe them away. She was surprised when the door opened, interrupting her half-hearted concentration.

"Good morning!" Ruth walked into the studio, smiling.

Laena looked up, not thinking anything good could be said about it. "Hello, Ruth. You are up early."

"And you look like you've been at this all night."

Laena nodded. "I couldn't sleep, so I came down here and got caught up with it all."

Ruth came closer and sat on the chair by the worktable. "The time has come for some plain speaking around here. First of all, this should be your last all-nighter, Laena."

Laena looked up, ready to deny her tiredness. Her back ached and she was exhausted. But the look on Ruth's face stopped her. Obviously, Ruth was not thinking about the work, but about Laena's health and the baby. She flushed as she realized that she had not been thinking about the baby when she ignored her body's demands for sleep. She nodded once, looking back down at the pot she made on the wheel.

"Why don't you clean up and I'll make us some breakfast?" Ruth offered softly.

Laena wiggled the fingers of her free hand, motioning for her attention.

Ruth looked at her.

Laena could see the worry in her face. "Please don't worry about me, Ruth. My being here shouldn't serve as a stressor for you."

Ruth didn't wait. "Look, Laena. Michael spilled the beans when I pushed him. Now, I don't know what is happening between you and Jack, and personally I want to knock him on the head but I will stay out of that part. What I will say is that this is my house, not his. I don't want you thinking that you have to leave. I love my son, but he hasn't lived here for almost…well, too many years for to think about now. And *you* have made me very happy, coming here and sharing the house with me. With you, Laena, I feel like I've rediscovered life again. Instead of winding down like so many people my age, you have helped me find new interests, get involved and even start dating once again. I'm sure most people would say I'm being an unnatural mother, but if push comes to shove, Laena, I want you to stay."

Laena stopped the wheel and stared at Ruth. "You can't choose me over Jack, Ruth. Your family would be up in arms. And maybe it would be better if I just left before things get any messier."

Ruth shook her head vehemently. "I want you to promise me that you won't make any decisions, one way or another for at least a month."

Laena hesitated for a few moments, but knew she owed this to Ruth. She nodded her head in agreement.

Ruth smiled. "Clean up and come to the house for breakfast."

Laena covered the pot with a damp cloth. Thankful for the installation of a full-size bathroom, she rinsed off her hands and forearms, drying off quickly. As she made her way to the house, she was totally aware of her aching back. No more marathon sessions on the wheel, she realized with a shrug.

When she entered the kitchen a few moments later, she found Ruth seated at the table, reading a note. Something about the look on Ruth's face told her it was from Jack and it didn't look like good news. She took the seat opposite the older woman and waited for her to speak.

"It's from Jack." Ruth held up the paper, turning it slightly.

Laena recognized his handwriting, nodding.

"He says he decided to head into the city and see about some of the job offers he has gotten recently."

Laena gasped, too quickly pressing her hand to her mouth to cover it. Her stomach was somersaulting. Hundreds of crazy, worrywart thoughts started bombarding her. "Does he say when he'll be home?" she asked softly, grateful that her voice didn't break.

"He isn't sure how long he will be, but he says he needs to make some decisions about the future."

Silence followed.

Laena finally swallowed hard and asked, "Why didn't he say goodbye?"

Ruth looked up from the note to meet Laena's gaze across the table.

Laena could see the older woman's concern in her expression.

"I imagine it was because he left at the crack of dawn. He used to do that on his visits here to miss traffic for the trip back into the city." Half under her breath she muttered, "It sounds to me as if he's running away from his decision."

Staring down at the table, Laena was afraid that if she met Ruth's gaze, she might lose it. She felt as though her heart broke, shattering into little fragments. Jack might have said in the note he planned on considering his business decisions, but she knew that he was really concerned whether he wanted to take on the responsibility of a new family at this stage in his life. She knew that he had obviously considered his procreation days at an end. And while some men might have chosen to reverse the surgery, or at least try, Jack hadn't even been given the choice. No doubt, he'd spent last night thinking.

"Well, I hope he finds something he will enjoy doing." Laena took a deep breath and forced a smile to her lips. "Enjoying your work is really important."

Ruth didn't say anything but crumpled the note in her fist, dropping it to the table. She stood, turning to the refrigerator. "I'll start breakfast, and then I'm putting you to bed!"

Laena heard Ruth muttering under her breath about blockheads, sons, and men in general. Once she was sure the older woman wouldn't see, she reached out and grabbed the crumpled piece of paper, stuffing it into her pants pocket to be perused later.

* * * * *

Several weeks later, Laena was in the studio working. She had the place to herself since Ruth had gone into town to meet Frank for lunch and a movie. Seated at the worktable, she pounded at some clay, taking out her frustrations. She wore one of Ruth's caftans. Almost overnight, her tummy had increased in size. Her jeans were too tight to fasten and while Ruth wanted her to go on a shopping spree for maternity clothes, she kept delaying the inevitable. As the first week of August passed, and if her dates were correct, she guessed she was five months along. But suddenly she looked like the pregnancy was a lot more. Ruth had been after her to call Michael and make an appointment, but she had been putting it off.

She ate very well, thanks to Ruth. And she was in bed by nine every night, again thanks to Ruth. Clearly Ruth was focused enough to think about the baby, which was logical, since it was her grandbaby! Even if Jack doubted her—

Suddenly she heard a noise at the open doorway and looked up. She gasped, seeing the last person she expected to see.

Jeff Hunt stepped through the open door and looked at his ex-wife. He knew it was a safe bet to come out here because the gossip all over town was about how Jack Spencer had taken off once again.

A moment later, Laena looked up from her work, smiling. "Where's the cat?" she asked softly.

It took Jeff a moment to catch the slur and he gritted his teeth. Typical of Laena to make some nasty comment, he thought to himself. "Is that anyway to talk to a guest?"

Laena looked away from Jeff and pounded the clay down hard onto the worktable again. "The difference is a guest is invited, and you were not."

Jeff clenched his teeth once again, fighting to keep from snapping back at Laena. She still had the tongue of a viper. "Look, I didn't come out here to exchange barbs with you, Laena."

Laena looked down at the clay and pounded it again. "All right. Why are you here?"

"I heard you were pregnant and wanted to see if it was true."

Laena glanced up at Jeff for a second, and then back to the table. "I'm surprised you didn't just look through Michael's files."

Jeff felt the heated flush moving up his neck, guilty that her words were so accurate. Damn!

"So, now you know. It's none of your business, by the way."

"True. I'm curious as to who the father is, seeing as how Jack was Michael's first vasectomy patient. I wouldn't have thought you would cuckold your lover just to get back at me. All you've done is made a fool of yourself." Jeff moved over to face Laena across the worktable. He folded his arms across his chest. "Unless of course you didn't know Jack had the vasectomy. In that case, I'm guessing your fooling around caught up with you." Rocking back on his heels, he guessed that he'd gotten the better of her on that one!

Laena sat for a moment, unmoving, before she looked up at her ex-husband, meeting his gaze. "I'm not like you, Jeff. I don't cheat, even if I'm not married. Whether Jack believes it or not, I've never been with anyone except him since our divorce. Now, will you please just go? You have your answer, and please go before Ruth comes down here. Your presence would upset her, considering her relationship with your father."

"I know for a fact that Ruth isn't here. She and Father had a luncheon date."

"So, that is why you snaked your way out here, huh?" Suddenly she felt really tired and didn't have the heart or energy to continue this verbal sparring. "Just go, Jeff. I'd like to be alone."

Jeff took a step towards the door. "You should get used to being alone, Laena. It appears as if Jack doesn't believe you, seeing as how he has made himself scarce lately."

Laena's breath caught at the sharp pain his words caused. It was true. Jack hadn't called or written since he had left almost four weeks earlier. She was pretty sure Ruth had talked to him a few times, but she hadn't said anything to Laena about it. She reached over to wet her hands and picked up the clay again. She had added too much water and the clay was a wet mushy mess. Angrily, she glanced back up at Jeff.

He started for the door, smiling. In less than a second or two, he was on his way towards his car.

Without thinking, Laena closed her fists into the wet, sloppy goop and stood to follow him.

Jeff was a few feet from his fancy convertible, when he turned to look back.

She saw the surprise on his face. Obviously, he had not expected her to follow him.

"Maybe you should get used to this," Jeff told her with a nasty grin.

Laena knew better, sensing her ex-husband needed to get still one more verbal spear into her back, but felt compelled to ask, "What?'

"Men walking away from you."

Feeling a little foggy, perhaps due to tiredness, she repeated her question, "What?"

"You stupid bitch—get used to being fucked and then dumped."

Laena didn't think, she only reacted. She threw the clay with exceedingly accurate aim. Maybe all those hours of playing ball with the kids paid off. The glob of wet clay smacked Jeff clearly in the middle of his chest, splattering onto his face and dripping down onto his expensive trousers, and—

Laena glanced down. Yes! He had on his Italian handmade leather loafers. She stayed still, waiting for him to react first.

The furious look in her ex-husband's eyes nearly shouted that he was ready to strike her for ruining his silk tie and expensive clothing.

Laena was stunned that she had acted so childishly. And yet she wanted to blast him with the other handful.

Suddenly, applause sounded from behind them.

Laena spun and saw that Jack stood at the side of the studio, clapping his hands.

He was dressed casually in jeans and T-shirt. He grinned and started walking towards her.

Laena didn't care who he applauded. She was too pissed at him for deserting her, and she let fly the other handful of clay. This one wasn't quite as accurate, but it did hit one arm and shoulder.

Jack looked surprised for a moment, but he didn't stop grinning. "Good shot, little mama." He stopped as he reached her side, holding her gaze for a long moment. He then turned to face Jeff. "You saved me from hitting him." He slid his arm around her shoulders, pulled her close. "Now, Jeff, for the sake of our families and future relations, I suggest you get the hell out of here before I succumb to the overwhelming need to alter your face."

Jeff glared at the older man.

Laena could see him pausing and thinking. She guessed Jeff had no doubt that if it came down to it, Jack probably could do him some serious damage.

He turned quickly and climbed into his car, cursing loudly when the clay dripped onto the plush light-colored interior. He started the car and gunned the engine, spewing dust behind him as he sped down the drive.

After a few moments, Jack turned Laena to face him with his hands on her shoulders. "I'm sorry, Laena. I should have come back sooner, and I can only blame it on cold feet. I used the job search as an excuse. I wasn't planning on being a new dad at the age of forty-eight, well, forty-nine when it actually comes. Here I faced a major career change and meeting you knocked me off my feet. None of that excuses my behavior. Learning that you were pregnant and realizing my surgery had failed was quite a shock to my system."

Laena nodded, showing that she understood that it was a shock. Still, she was experiencing the rush of surprise that he was finally home. Added to that was anger at being deserted without a word. And there was the fact that he had not spoken to her during his phone calls. She opened her mouth to speak.

Jack covered her lips with his index finger. "Shh, let me finish, honey. I missed you like hell all the while I was gone. I wouldn't blame you if you kicked dirt in my face, or hit me with more clay." He chuckled softly. "But even if you did, I wouldn't give up or leave. I would hang around you until you felt sorry enough for me to give me a second chance."

Laena laughed, but the smile didn't reach her eyes. "I don't want you to come back because of the baby. No one is ever happy when that happens."

Jack pulled her close and wrapped his arms around her. "I don't think this feels like 'caring just because of the baby', does it?"

Laena felt heat rush through her as his arousal pressed against her. While only a few weeks had passed, it seemed longer. She lifted her face and met his mouth eagerly, kissing him back as hotly and as passionately as ever before. More than anything, she wanted to say something sexy like "Let's go make use of that nice long sofa in the studio". But she needed to tell him things that had been preying on her mind since he'd left. She eased away from him.

Jack grinned. "I've been thinking about making slow, tender love to you." He grabbed Laena's hand and led her back to the studio. He kicked the door shut as he yanked his shirt over his head. He backed Laena to the sofa and his fingers were making quick work of the small buttons down the front of the caftan. He stopped about halfway down and looked into her eyes.

"I don't want to object to your taste in clothes, honey. But this looks like something my mom would wear."

Laena could feel the heat stain her cheeks. "It is your mother's. I don't have anything that fits at the moment."

Jack released the last button and moved his hands to rest on her shoulders. "And I guess running around naked didn't seem like a good idea, huh?"

Laena laughed. "You haven't seen me naked lately or you wouldn't need to ask that."

"Sweetheart, I know you are beautiful, and you will only become more so." His hands began pushing the caftan off her shoulders.

Instinctively, Laena raised her hands to cover herself.

Jack pushed the dress off her shoulders so only her crossed arms held it partially up. His hands curled around hers and he slowly pulled them down. Then he felt her resistance and looked up.

Tears were running down her cheeks.

"Oh, God, honey! What's wrong? Are you all right?"

Laena pulled the caftan back up, holding the front edges together with one hand. "I'm still ticked at you," she muttered as the tears threatened to choke her words.

"I'm sorry, Laena. I handled everything wrong. Mother kept telling me over the phone I was going about this all-wrong and I should be talking to you. But I wanted to present you with a definite future. I needed to show you that I could care for you and the baby, even though I wasn't a scrappy kid with twenty years to plan for college and so on." He pulled her into his arms, holding her gently.

Laena let go of the dress and curled her arms around him, cuddling her head onto his chest. The sound of his heartbeat, thudding strongly beneath her ear was reassuring and soothing to her frazzled nerves. "I thought you'd...damn it! I don't even know that I could think rationally anymore. My temper is so short. I can't believe that I actually threw clay at you and Jeff. How immature! What kind of mother am I going to be?"

"Hmm, a good ball-playing one, that's for sure!"

Laena pulled away, lightly pounding one fist on his chest. "Just what a girl needs to know these days!"

"A modern one does, anyway. Now, go ahead and tell me what else is bothering you. Just let it all come out."

Laena bit her tongue to hold back the words that she loved him. But she still felt that she wasn't sure about his… commitment. Was he really sure that he wanted to take on a new family at this age? Part of her wanted to ask him outright. Yet a little voice told her to wait and take every single moment with him that she could get. Memories might be all she had to cling to in the future. She met his gaze.

Jack's hands lifted, curving to either side of her face, cradling it tenderly. Leaning into her, he kissed her lips lightly. "I'm sorry for acting like such a jerk. I guess age doesn't improve us for all the challenges we face in life."

"I know. I've had some trouble adjusting to the thought of motherhood. Even though I wanted to have a child with Jeff, since the divorce and with the way I was feeling about men in general, it didn't seem like much of a possibility. You pretty much knocked me off my feet." She paused, half-afraid she'd revealed too much with her last statement.

"Laena, honey, that feeling was mutual. When I came home last Christmas, I was finishing out eight years of nonstop adrenaline rush and stress-producing work. My plan was to relax for a few days, and then finish out the term. After that, I figured I would settle down here for a while, spend time with my family and let the world go by without me in it. And then I saw you."

Her gaze met his. Easily she recalled the heart-racing, breathless encounters of those first few days. Suddenly she wanted him more than ever. Maybe this was just pregnancy hormones, or abstinence. None of that mattered as she stepped away from him, slipping the caftan from her shoulders.

Jack lowered his gaze to watch as the dress slid down and finally off her body, pooling at her feet. He was a little surprised to find she was completely naked. And then he realized that she probably didn't have underpants that fit either. He made a mental note that tomorrow they would go shopping.

He could feel her nervousness as if it were a tangible thing. Gazing at her body, highlighted by the afternoon sunlight coming through the windows and skylight, he marveled at how truly beautiful she was. His eyes lowered to her breasts and he saw that some of her weight gain had been delightfully distributed evenly between them. He took a step closer, unable to resist the lure of touching her.

Laena stood uncertainly, fighting the almost overwhelming urge to cover herself with her hands. She stared intently at Jack's face, wanting to read his thoughts as he looked at her body. She had seen in her own mirror the changes that had occurred so far. And she had not felt in the least bit attractive lately. She gasped as Jack lifted his hands and covered her large, tender breasts with his hands. Her nipples were already peaked and poked at the palms of his hands.

Tenderly, Jack just held her sensitive flesh for a moment. And then, he began a sensual and slow massage of her full breasts. Jack looked into her eyes, smiling as he continued to massage her breasts. "Now this is nice. I've got even more to play with now."

Laena giggled nervously, but stopped as he started to pluck at her nipples. "Now it isn't just my bras that don't fit," she whispered softly.

"Hmm, such lovely big tits, it would be a crime to bind them." He lowered his head and took one nipple into his mouth. His sucking was gentle but firm and a moment later she had to grab at Jack's arms as her legs buckled. He pressed her back onto the sofa and quickly removed his jeans before he lowered himself to lie beside her. He cupped her breast, resuming his erotic massage. He leaned down and kissed her parted lips, their tongues meeting and dancing.

His hand slid down to stroke over her rounded belly. He explored her flesh slowly before he slid his hand to the apex of her thighs. He growled low in his throat and murmured appreciatively, "Smooth like silk."

Her wetness made it easy to slide one finger between the folds to her clit. Soft, gentle flicks to begin with, and he coaxed her passionate response from her very depths. Soon he slid two fingers inside her tight channel, adding increased teasing and massage.

Lastly, he returned to her nipples, sucking them intermittently. Back and forth he would go, taking his time to pleasure each nipple. Long pulling motions with his mouth, circling each nipple with his tongue. "I love your nipples, honey. Long, thick and responsive. Sucking your nipple is amazing. When I pull away, there is always a loud 'plop' sound when you leave my mouth."

Laena couldn't stop or hold back her body's response to his words. Letting the words replay in her brain, she cried out loudly, "Yes, oh my God!"

Jack jerked his head in surprise as her body trembled in passionate response. He didn't pause, though, and immediately worked her flesh to a second and then a third climax. His hand was wet as he dragged it back up her body, spreading her wetness over her distended flesh. He moved to lie above her, keeping his weight suspended with his arms.

Without a word, Laena moved her legs farther apart. When he held himself away for a few more seconds, she lifted her legs and wrapped them around him. She tightened her thighs and pulled him closer. He resisted for a moment only and then thrust his hard cock deep into her wet and eager channel.

Laena cried out as he filled her body. She curled her fingers into his muscular chest, whispering softly, "Fuck me, Jack, please."

Jack still held back. He was concerned about the baby and was fighting the nearly overwhelming urge to sink into her flesh hard and fast, over and over. He groaned harshly. "I need to be careful, honey," he told her softly. "Did you ask Michael if it was safe to have sex?" Jack's arms shook with the strain of holding back.

Laena tightened her legs around Jack. "I haven't been back to ask him. Ruth gave me several books to read. Oh, God! Up to eight months…this is okay. Jack, please, I need you."

Her softly spoken words and hot flesh were too much.

Jack started thrusting in and out of her eager, needy body. Each time he pulled back, her channel seemed to tighten and hold him within for a moment or two. Jack tried to go slow, but it was too much. He moved his hand between them and worked her clit to her fourth orgasm.

As he felt her contractions take over, he let himself jerk into her body hard and fast. He thrust forward once more and shot his seed deep into her body.

Even as his passion washed through him, Jack was still amazed with the reality his seed had made the baby in her belly. It was real. He was a daddy all over again, and he liked the warm feeling he got deep down inside. Starting to collapse onto her body, he caught himself and slid to the side at the last second. He closed his eyes, listening to Laena breathing beside him. After a few moments, as his heart calmed and his breathing slowed, he lifted his eyelids to look at her face. He saw the rosy flush on her cheeks and the sweat-dampened curls that clung to the sides of her face. He lifted one hand to caress down the side of her cheek.

Laena turned to look at Jack and smiled. She spoke quickly. "Wow!"

Jack laughed. "My thoughts exactly, honey." He moved his hand down and cupped her nearest breast. He enjoyed the feeling of the full, firm globe overflowing his hand. "I missed you, Laena."

Laena took a deep breath. "Me, too." She yawned and her eyelids drifted shut. It was just a moment later and she had fallen asleep.

Jack watched her as she slept, her body curling towards him a few moments later. He shifted to hold her close. He would have to tell her about his job-hunting expedition. But all that could wait. The first priority would be a trip to the doctor, followed by an extensive shopping trip. He slid off the sofa and covered her with a soft blanket. After he dressed, he walked up to the house. He called Michael and set up an appointment for first thing in the morning. He made one more call and then started back towards the studio.

As he reached the door, he heard a car pulling into the long drive. Turning, he saw his mother driving her sporty convertible. He grinned and waved. Pointing towards the studio, he walked into the studio and awakened Laena slowly, helping her to dress once again. They walked back to the house together with Jack's arm curved around her back.

All the way back, he let his gaze roam over the house. He recalled how much his father had wanted him to carry on here, at the farm. But he had had his own dreams and those involved law school and possibly politics. Almost thirty years had passed since his arguments over his future with his father, and here he was, back living in his parents' house. This could be a strange world at times.

He resolved that he would speak to David once more. This time he'd let him know not only would he enthusiastically support his decision, but if he wanted to take classes part-time, he would pay for that as well. Strange how easy it was to forget what it was like when you were young and had dreams you wanted to pursue. Undoubtedly, he owed a lot of his father's change of mind to his mother. He had turned out all right. No doubt, David would as well. Jack pressed a kiss to Laena's forehead, feeling incredibly happy just then.

Chapter Sixteen

Laena felt self-conscious as they entered the doctor's office the following morning. She didn't have anything to wear, so she'd borrowed a pair of pants which had stretch waistbands from Ruth. A shirt was a problem and she had ended up wearing one of Jack's T-shirts.

Jack had told her their next stop would be the store. He went back with her when her name was called, ignoring her glare.

Laena turned her back to Jack as she shed her clothes and pulled on the gown. She got up on the end of the table and sat there, her feet dangling. She ignored Jack, who grinned at her the whole time.

Michael came in a moment later. He smiled at Laena, but gave a startled jerk of real surprise when he saw his brother sitting there as well. He looked back to Laena. "I had decided to give you a few more days and then I would come out to pay you a visit. I told you to see me. I thought you understood it should be soon."

Laena flushed. "I know, but things have been—"

Jack interrupted her, "She's here now, so none of that matters."

Michael nodded and started his examination.

Laena stayed quiet because Jack had more than enough questions for them both. She sat up finally, relieved that it was over.

Michael took a large Styrofoam cup from one of the cupboards in the exam room, filling it with water. As he held it out towards her, he instructed her. "Get started on that, Laena. I want to do an ultrasound, and you need a full bladder." Michael handed her the glass. "Refill it as soon as this one is done."

Laena started drinking the water.

Jack stood. "What time do you think you'll be ready to start, Mike? I have a few errands I could run and save Laena waiting on me once we'd finished here."

Michael grinned. "Considering the average time, I'd say you have an hour."

After learning how long, Jack winked at Laena. "I'm guessing that you want to shop another day, right?"

Laena nodded, his perceptiveness catching her off-guard.

"Happy drinking, honey. I'll get a few things out of the way." He kissed her lightly, and then left.

So, she sat alone, drinking two big glasses of water. A nurse popped in as she finished the second, smiled and told her to do one more. A little over an hour passed before Jack came back.

Not more than a few minutes passed before the door opened to admit one of Michael's staff, pushing the ultrasound machine. Michael came a few moments later.

Laena was soon lying on the table with her rounded belly exposed for the world to see. She joked lightly, hoping it would make her feel better. "I feel like a beached whale."

Michael laughed. "This will be cold," he told her, squirting conducting gel on her lower stomach. "It will sound a little strange at first."

A few moments later, the room was filled with a "sloshing" sound.

Jack leaned over and kissed her forehead. "Not a whale, honey. More like a dolphin." He laughed when she stuck out her tongue.

Jack moved so they could both see the monitor.

Laena stared at the screen, unable to tell what anything was. She half-heard Jack asking more questions and Michael answering them. She heard when the sloshing became louder and Michael pointed out that was the baby's heartbeat. He asked her to turn to one side, then the other and finally again on her back. She was mesmerized by the sound and barely registered Michael's surprised, half-choked shout. She looked up and Jack had moved closer to the screen. She felt tightness in her throat. "Is something wrong? Is the baby okay?"

Michael turned to smile and told her where to look on the screen. He began moving the sensor device on her belly again. Slowly he pointed out one foot, and then another.

Laena smiled seeing the tiny feet.

But then Michael pointed to a third foot.

Her heart seemed to stop. "Something's wrong with the baby? Why are there three feet? What's going on?"

Michael grinned. "No, Laena. Look, here's the other foot. That makes four—" He paused, and then he readjusted the sensor so it displayed one heart beating. "There's the heartbeat, and if you'll turn towards me a little…"

Then Laena saw the second heart beating. In disbelief, she watched as Michael slowly pointed out two heads, and at least three hands. Then the babies shifted again. That's when Laena saw one of them sucking its thumb! Four hands. Four feet. She took a deep breath and let it out slowly. Two babies…her stomach turned a somersault. Fear filled her, followed by a growing sense of wonder. Two! How was she to cope with two babies when the thought of one still scared the bejeebers out of her!

Jack looked from the screen to Laena. "Can you tell the sex yet?"

Michael shook his head. "I've tried to see, but they won't spread apart enough."

Jack laughed. "Must be girls then." He laughed even harder when Laena huffed testily. "Two girls will be perfect since we already have two boys."

Laena felt a roaring in her ears. Warmth filled her inner being at his words. Apparently, he was thinking of them as a family already. He had so easily said "we" have two boys. She quickly brushed the tears from her eyes and tried to focus on what the two brothers were saying.

But Michael was already turning off the machine. His assistant wiped her belly and offered to help her sit up.

The rest of the appointment passed quickly and she soon was back in the car with Jack, the videotape resting on the seat between them. He asked her once more about going shopping, but Laena shook her head.

In the car, Jack tried several times to start a conversation. Each question was answered with only one word. He gave up, and they drove home in silence.

As soon as the car stopped, Laena jumped out and went straight to the studio.

Ruth had just come out and saw Laena going into the studio. She looked towards her son.

Jack climbed from the car, the videotape in his hand.

Ruth saw it and asked immediately, "Is everything all right?"

Jack heard the worry in his mother's voice. He smiled and nodded reassurance. "It's all in how you look at it, I guess. Everything is normal, for two babies."

Ruth yelped in joyful surprise. She rushed down the steps and hugged Jack close. "Twins! How wonderful!"

Jack returned his mother's embrace. "I'm not so sure Laena is of the same opinion, Mom. She hasn't said more than a few words since we found out."

"She is probably just feeling a little overwhelmed. I remember that Celia was a little numb at first. I'll go and talk to her."

Jack reached for his mother's arm. "I should go."

Ruth shook her head. "You can't understand how a woman feels when she is pregnant, dear. Let me go. We won't be long, and we'll come back up to the house."

When Jack still held onto her arm, Ruth turned back towards her oldest son. "I promise you. Why don't make us tea and cut some of the cake I made? We'll be up to join you in about ten minutes or so."

* * * * *

Laena looked up as Ruth entered the studio. She had grabbed some clay and kneaded it on the table. "Hi, Ruth. Did Jack send you down here?"

Ruth sat across from Laena. "No, he wanted to come, but I told him it would be better if I came to talk with you. He told me the news."

Laena looked up from the clay. "You didn't say great news."

"Well, women tend to see these things differently from men."

Laena laughed shortly. "Yes. Jack and Michael were crowing about it. All I could think of was how can I manage two when thinking about one has me scared?"

Ruth smiled at the younger woman. "I felt the same way when I was pregnant with Jack. And Celia was quite bowled over when she learned she was having twin boys. And even though I'm sure he doesn't remember it, Jack wasn't all that excited in the beginning, either. Celia called me several times on the phone, worried Jack wouldn't be able to cope. But they both came around, and I went and stayed for a while until they got a routine established. And with you being here, we'll have no trouble coping with two babies." She reached over and covered Laena's hands with her own.

Laena smiled slowly, sniffling.

Ruth patted the younger woman's hands. "I think of you as my daughter, Laena. You and I have become very close, in spite of the difference in our ages. I want to be there for you, as you have been for me when I needed help. Now," Ruth pulled a hankie from her pocket. "Let's wipe away our tears and go have some tea. I made a cake while you were gone, so we can sample that as well."

When the two women entered the kitchen a few minutes later, they found Jack was already there, fixing the tea and munching on a piece of cake.

He turned guiltily when his mother called his name. Jack grinned and shrugged. "I never could resist one of your cakes."

Once they were all sitting around the table, Jack started talking. "First, I still owe you an apology, Laena, for taking off like I did. But the crux of the matter is that I've settled my next career. You'll have nothing to worry about whether I can provide for you and our babies."

Ruth stared at her son. "I know you've had lots of offers, both to speak and do the graduation circuit. Phillip said you'd had several very lucrative offers from DC firms, which have talked partnerships. On the news, they reported that you were approached to practice by an international law firm. My preference would be for you to stay here, but I don't want to unduly influence you, dear."

Jack grinned at his mother. "Duly noted, Mother." He paused and covered Laena's hands with his. "What is your opinion, Laena? I know I'm doing this back-ass-wards, and I should have told you my offers sooner."

Laena shook her head. She knew from things Ruth had said that Jack had offerings from some very large and influential law firms, not to mention the speaking engagements he could accept. And here he was now, almost proudly announcing that he would stay here. She had no doubt the decision was due solely to her being pregnant. "Ruth mentioned some things, but it is really your choice, Jack. So long as you are happy, that is what matters. People need to enjoy what they do."

"Thank you, Laena. I saw Tony Banks around a few weeks back and we chatted for a while. Tony talked about how he had a pretty hectic law practice, being the only attorney in the surrounding area." Jack sipped his tea, looking from his mother to Laena.

Laena couldn't shake the feeling that more existed to this than met the eye, or the ear, in this case.

"I can see you are surprised," Jack said a few seconds later.

Ruth cleared her throat. "Is this a done deal?"

Jack looked from his mother to Laena. "You mean, can I back out and go with one of the more lucrative offers?"

"Yes, Jack. I know you've had some pretty amazing offers." Ruth nodded, frowning deeply.

Laena remembered that Ruth had talked about how Jack had met with all the large firms, been wined and dined and generally courted like a plum catch. She had no doubt that Jack would be a prime asset to any of the large law firms and would have joined as a full partner. His name would have been quite a coup to add to any letterhead. She couldn't help but feel that he made this decision for the wrong reasons. It was obvious that Ruth thought it was wrong, even though she had expressed a wish to have him near to home. That he decided to join an old family friend's law practice in town sounded suspiciously like a last-ditch solution to an unexpected problem.

A moment later, Jack touched the side of her face.

Startled, she realized she'd been shaking it. "You shouldn't settle for this. I'm sure the financial difference will be huge. Don't you want to travel, live in the big city and have the entire hubbub and so on? You've lived in the spotlight for a long time —"

"There's no need to be shaking your head or wagging your finger me, Laena." He reached out and grabbed the finger she'd started to point at him. "I know precisely what I'm doing. I know you're both shocked, as I'm sure the others will be as well. Even Tony, grateful as he is, still doubts my sanity. And money isn't everything, sweetheart, but don't go worrying about money. I have it all figured out on paper for you to see."

"Now that sounds like my son," Ruth spoke softly, covering her eldest son's hand. "But I'm sure you'll spend a lot of time explaining your decision to people."

Jack held Laena's gaze for a long moment before he looked at his mother. "True, Mom. But the last eight years have taught me how precious family is, and how much I have missed by being gone. When the boys were young, I was always working. I know it was hard on Celia, even though she never complained. I'm not making the same mistakes this time."

Laena felt that she had to let him know what she thought. "Jack, I would never prevent you from seeing your child...I mean, children." She stopped, not liking how her words sounded.

Jack nodded. "I know, honey. But I want to be home, and I know how it can be in the large firms. I also don't want my kids growing up in the city. And unless Mom kicks us out, I'd like to stay here."

Laena felt her heart catch. He hadn't said anything about marriage, and to be honest, she wasn't sure she would say yes even if he did ask. She couldn't imagine how horrible going through another divorce would be, and this one would be complicated by children. Still, he talked about them being together and living as a family. For her, that was enough for now. She smiled slowly, aware that Ruth watched her, as well as Jack. "I don't care what you do, Jack, so long as you are happy doing it. Money doesn't matter that much, so long as everyone is happy." She repeated her assurances.

Jack grinned. "You don't need to worry about me putting food in my children's mouths, Laena. I won't go into details now, but financially we'll be fine. Tony and I have looked at it pretty seriously. The work is definitely too much for one lawyer, and probably could be handled by one and half. What we want to do is make it so we both have the hours we want. If we both end up working three-quarters, we'll be happy. Tony loves to fish, and he complained that he never has the free time. His kids are in school and he wants to make sure he's there for them." He stood and started clearing the dishes away. "Any questions?"

Ruth laughed. "See, Laena. He is already well-trained, so I think we should consider keeping him around the house after all."

They all laughed heartily and then went about cleaning up. For now, the subject was closed.

* * * * *

Jack looked at the closed door to Laena's bedroom. All day long he had continued to feel that something wasn't right between the two of them. Proof had come after dinner when Laena excused herself to go up to bed. There were no sly glances or quick smiles in his direction, which in the past had been her signals for him to follow her, soon. He stayed in the living room with his mother for another two hours, watching television and talking.

Ruth stood finally. "I'm off to bed. Suit yourself if you want to stay up longer. I have a date with Frank tomorrow. We'll be leaving early, around nine, and going into Richmond for some shopping and dinner. If we're running late, we'll stay over and drive back on Sunday."

Jack got up from the sofa. He idly checked the door and began turning off lights. "Is it time for me to have a talk with Frank about his intentions towards you?" he asked laughingly.

Ruth shook her head. "No, you will not. And don't let your sisters know about this either."

Jack kissed his mother's cheek as they came to the stairs. Her bedroom was halfway down the hall. "I won't. Promise."

That was thirty minutes ago. After a long time in the shower, taking extra time to shave, it ended with cold water, which didn't help dissipate his desire one iota. More than anything, he wanted to go in and join Laena in bed. But he had little doubt that she was sound asleep by now. Turning, he walked the short distance to his room and paused outside the door.

"I thought I left the door open," he spoke quietly. Shrugging, he grasped the knob and turned it. Nothing happened. "What the fuck!" The damned door was locked. How could that have happened? More importantly, where was the key?

He turned quickly to go downstairs when he realized that he only had a small towel in his hand. Since his mother was downstairs and in bed, he had not taken a robe with him into the bathroom. Afterwards, he had dried completely, grabbing a small hand towel for his hair. Sighing heavily in frustration, he started for the stairs.

Laena's bedroom door was now opened slightly, and a faint light came from within.

Jack stopped. He was sure her door was closed when he'd passed earlier. Maybe one of the old keys was in her door. He could use it to open his bedroom. Pleased with himself for thinking of the solution, he stepped over to Laena's bedroom. As quietly as possible, he gently eased open her door. He hoped it wouldn't creak. Maybe he could get his hand around and check—

"If you've come to rob me, kind sir, you are ill-clothed for your endeavor," Laena spoke from her bed.

Jack's head turned first. He felt like a naughty schoolboy.

"Don't worry. I'm not the Mother Superior coming to teach a recalcitrant boy his proper manners," she added.

He saw that she was unable to keep from smiling. He slowly came into the room and saw she watched him closely.

Her gaze moved down, and then very slowly, almost as if she were inspecting for something, it came back up.

Starting to speak, he had to clear his throat first. "It appears the wind blew my bedroom door shut and somehow the damned door locked." Taking a couple of steps towards the bed, his gaze moved over her.

Her blonde hair was curled over her shoulders. She wore some kind of frothy, filmy pale pink negligee. He could tell the bra was lace and her breasts spilled out of it big time. It was obviously pre-pregnancy because the satiny material stretched tautly across her rounded belly. Lying on her side, one leg slid forward, and kept moving up and down against the other one.

It wasn't easy, but he forced his gaze to meet hers. "I thought you'd be asleep."

"I dozed for a little, but I felt restless. You know the feeling...kind of itchy, all over. So I took a shower and shaved." Laena paused to rub the top foot up and down the calf of the other leg again. "Then I even put on lotion, all over my body. But it just didn't seem to help."

Jack felt his body reacting still further to her words. If she looked down, she'd have no doubt as to what he needed scratched.

"I wondered if you could help."

Jack coughed. "Uhm, sure, Laena, what do you need?"

"I had a few places I couldn't get covered too well, and I wondered if you would put on the lotion for me. Please?"

"Well, sure, of course. Where is the bottle?" he asked, walking to the side of the bed. If she still didn't show any interest when he was done, he promised himself that he would leave her to sleep alone tonight. After all, she needed a lot of sleep, he was sure.

"Here!" Laena said and tossed him a small bottle.

He watched in surprise.

As quick as firefly, she slipped off the long robe and kneeled with her back to him, at the edge of the bed. One, two, three...the straps were slipped off, her hair pulled to the side and she looked up at him, over her shoulder.

God damn! Jack thought. Laena was a born seductress. Sighing heavily, he filled his hands with the cream and began applying it to her back. He covered the whole area, except what was hidden by the lower rear section of the short nightgown. "How is that?" he asked, surprised at the hoarseness in his voice.

"That feels much better, but there is still another place."

"Just name it."

Laena turned slowly to look up.

He watched as one of her hands lifted.

Hope rose, as did his cock, when her hand neared his body. Instead, she moved a little more and slipped her fingers between her breasts. A second later, she pulled out an antique-styled key ring.

"I think this might be the cause of the problem." She tossed the ring onto the floor and then pulled the cups of the negligee straight down. Her breasts popped free.

"Damn, woman! I think you are trying to kill me!" Jack took a deep breath. "Do you have any idea how sexy — ?"

She slid her hands beneath her breasts, lifting them upwards. "Surely you don't mean these, kind sir? I wouldn't have thought a gentleman such as you would dishonor himself by speaking of a woman's — "

Jack laughed as he put one knee on the bed beside her. "Tits? Boobs?"

"Sir! I mean my womanly blooms!"

He pushed her back onto the bed.

Laena's hands fell to her sides and she smiled up at him. "Do you have plans for my blossoms?"

Jack put more lotion in the palm of one hand. As he rubbed his hands together, he spoke. "You could say that, for sure. I am going to rub my palms over these luscious beauties until you are crying out for me to suck your nipples."

"God, Jack, stop talking and just do it!" She grabbed his wrists, pulling him onto the bed more fully.

Jack grinned at her eagerness. "Never let it be said that I kept a lady waiting!" He promptly placed his hands on her breasts, massaging the cream in with varying strengths of motion.

Laena closed her eyes and moaned softly.

"My lady likes this, does she?"

"Hmm."

"Well, if the lady will turn over, I will happily finish her back." Jack offered, still not removing his hands though. He was sure he could see the indecision on her face.

After nearly half a minute, she turned over.

Jack grabbed the cream and squirted it liberally over her skin.

"Ooh! Cold!"

"I'll take care of that," he promised. Slowly he began rubbing his hands over her upper back once again. The cream eased his way down her back. At her sides, he ran his hands from mid-back down to her hips and back up. Finally, he slid his hands onto her ass cheeks. He massaged her quietly for a long time, and then with one move he ran them down onto her thighs.

Her legs parted, giving him plenty of space to do her inner thighs.

Jack went straight down her legs to her feet. He spent a long time on each foot. Without any warning, he went from sliding his hands around her ankles for the sixth time to straight up and in.

"Oh, my God!" Laena yelped in surprise as his hands further parted her legs.

"What do you know? There is already some moisture here...I don't think it's your moisturizing cream, honey."

"You win! I give up!" Laena muttered into the bedcovers.

Jack moved his fingers across her pussy lips, feeling their slick moisture. He leaned down, resting against her back for a few moments. Whispering, he said, "If I do this correctly, my love, we will both win."

Laena groaned as he slid two fingers inside her. A second later, another finger eased onto her clit. Wiggling and pressing against the erotic bud, he massaged her G-spot. She knew this wasn't going to last long. For the last two hours, she'd been up here fantasizing about what she would say and do. Her whole body was in overdrive.

"Can you lift up onto your knees?"

Laena heard him ask her through her sensual fog. Nodding, she pushed with her hands, and soon had her bottom in the air.

Jack's hands shifted her slightly, and then he resumed his erotic massage. The bed shifted as he got to his feet.

Laena wiggled her butt, wanting him to finish what he'd started. "God! Jack!" she cried out impatiently.

"I know, darling." His fingers intensified and increased speed. He barely pulled free and thrust inside her.

"Yes!" Laena sobbed as he entered her, and after just a few thrusts, her body orgasmed hard. Her whole body shook. The only thing keeping her upright was his hand. Through the insanity of explosions going on inside her, she was dimly aware of Jack's continued thrusts. Each spasm of her cunt dragged and pulled against his thrusts. She tried to tighten and hold him, but it was impossible. Through the dimness of her remaining consciousness, she felt Jack speed up and shorten his thrusts. Soon he jerked forward, pressing and holding her tightly. She felt his seed exploding inside her.

"I'd love to stay inside you, love, but I don't want to crush you or the babies," Jack murmured to her softly a minute later, pulling free of her body. He stood at the side of the bed. "Crawl up here and get under the covers, Laena. I'll turn off the light."

When he got back, she was settled under the sheet and blankets. The dim light from her bathroom highlighted his face as he returned. She watched him climb in beside her.

He took several moments to settle. He didn't immediately spoon her, as he often did.

But then, she reminded herself, she was lying on her back.

"You must be tired, Laena. Throwing pots, throwing clay at ex-husbands and lovers and now seduction. Whew! I'd say that's a busy two days for a pregnant lady."

She couldn't tell if he was serious or teasing her. Immediately, she rolled onto her side to frown at him.

Jack grinned.

Instead of the snappy remark she'd thought of, she instead said what had been on her mind since his return. "Are you sure about this decision? It seems so dull compared to the other offers you could pursue. I know you are doing this because you feel responsible." She ended with a gesture towards her lower abdomen.

Jack laughed softly, rolling onto his side to look at her. "I am responsible, just as you are. We made those two babies in your belly. Responsibility is not a dirty word in my book. We may not be anyone's ideal couple. We have the age difference—"

"How old are you, Jack? It's not nice to make a woman discuss her age, but I'm nearly thirty-six, which isn't much at all in my opinion. I mean lots of people of different ages—" Laena stopped abruptly. She'd almost said, "Marry." Jack hadn't yet brought up that topic. To be honest, she was still unsure about getting married again, even now that she was pregnant.

Last night she was still dealing with the idea of one baby, and now today she adjusted to the idea that she carried two babies. She wasn't panicking every hour. Ruth had spent a lot of time reassuring her. Still, she was an unmarried woman, soon to be an unwed mama. Not at all how she had planned to straighten out her life and get it back on track!

"So, the years don't matter?" Jack asked her softly.

Laena shook her head, partly to clear her head and the other to let him know it didn't make a difference to her. "We've been doing pretty well so far. My parents were in their sixties when I entered college."

"Hey." Jack reached over and gently brushed the strands of hair that clung to the sides of her face. "Tell me about your family. The couple of times I've asked you in the past, you managed to distract me."

Laena felt her cheeks flush. That was exactly what she'd done to avoid telling about her past. "I don't have any family left, Jack. Both of my parents are gone. They were both only children."

"God! You must have thought my family was a zoo!"

Shaking her head, she laughed. "Not completely. I soon learned all the animals' names and what to feed them. The only one to give me any trouble was the big silverback gorilla. His chest-thumping sucked me in."

Jack's laughter made her smile.

"You have the only chest I have any desire to do anything with, and thumping ain't it." He reached out and cupped her nearest breast, pushing the sheet down to her waist. Soon he narrowed his attention to her nipple, circling it with the tip of his finger. He flicked it several times. "Now, that might pass for thumping. Hmm, I'm thumping your nipple. Thump, thump."

Laena reached down and stopped him. "No. That reminds me of the rabbit. You know, the baby deer and...not sexy."

"Got it." Jack slid down his hand, pushing the sheet out of the way, exposing her rounded tummy. He rubbed her belly a few times and then leaned down. "Good night, babies." He pressed a light kiss to her tummy. Pulling back the sheets, he settled on his side. "Want to spoon?"

Laena blinked her eyes quickly to clear away the tears that had formed at Jack's impromptu actions. "Yeah, let's spoon." His warmth relaxed her completely, and she fell asleep minutes later.

Chapter Seventeen

With less than two months to go, Laena and Ruth walked through the department store, browsing the baby section. Laena wore a lovely maternity dress, enjoying the day in town with Ruth. Lunch had been a raucous event with Jack at a small, quaint restaurant near the building where his law practice was located.

Over lunch, the topic of nurseries and furniture had arisen. Jack had been quite supportive of the idea. When Laena accused him of just being glad of escaping a shopping trip, his guilty flush told the truth.

Almost as soon as they entered the only large department store in town, Ruth had seen something of interest and darted off, leaving Laena alone in the aisle, looking at different kinds of layette styles. Hearing a noise, she looked up and gasped when she saw Arlene walking towards her. Laena noticed that Arlene didn't have her son with her. Forcing a smile to her tense lips, she reminded herself to be nice and greeted the other woman. "Hello, Arlene."

Laena knew instantly by the look on the other woman's face that she was shocked, and not in a good way. Laena wondered if she knew about Jack, and her own pregnancy?

"Laena, what a surprise!" Arlene spoke, her voice a little high-pitched.

Laena nodded, feeling awkward and not knowing what to say. "I'm just looking for a few things for a nursery. I have to set it up pretty soon."

Arlene's gaze fell to her stomach.

Laena was intensely aware of her gaze. She stood awkwardly, wondering where the dickens Ruth had disappeared. In the back of her mind, she had known these kinds of meetings would be inevitable since they were staying here. The reality of living through one was something different. A little magic dust would come in handy right now she fantasized, recalling one of the children's books Jack had purchased. She'd begun reading them herself, to find her personal favorite.

Arlene nodded, folding her arms. "It does seem to go so slow at first, and then its like 'whoosh' and there is no time left for getting ready. You had just better *be* ready. When are you due?"

"According to Michael, he guesses around Christmas. He thinks I will probably deliver early."

Arlene picked up something and turned it over in her hands. "Really? Why does he think that? Have you had problems?"

Laena shook her head. "I'm having twins. So, he told me to be ready early." She stopped, seeing the startled jerk of the other woman's hand as she dropped the object. "You didn't even know I was pregnant, did you, Arlene?" Suddenly, perception flooded through her. Jeff, the idiot, had not bothered to tell his wife that his ex-wife was not only still in town and living with Ruth, but was pregnant.

When the other woman shook her head, Laena couldn't help but feel sorry for her. No one really likes surprises except on their birthday. Laena touched Arlene's arm in sympathy. "I'm sorry. But really, not many people know. I haven't been in town at all, and no one outside the family knows."

Arlene nodded tersely. "I'm sure Ruth told Frank, though, and I'm sure he told Jeff. I'm just surprised Jeff didn't tell me."

Laena bit her tongue. She knew nothing good come from her telling the other woman that her husband had known for a while. Instead, she shrugged nonchalantly. "You know how men are. They never think to tell us about that kind of stuff, unless it affects them. And he probably didn't want to bring up my name to you, considering the divorce and all."

Arlene started to say something, but stopped abruptly.

Laena turned and saw Ruth coming down the aisle towards them. From the look on Ruth's face, she appeared like an avenging angel swooping down on a mission. Laena smiled at Ruth, hoping to head her off. "Look who I ran into Ruth! We've just been exchanging a few tidbits of gossip. Did you find what you were looking for?"

Laena watched as Ruth paused, looking from Arlene's tense face to her smiling one. Ruth's surprise was obvious that it was Arlene who felt at a disadvantage, and not Laena.

Ruth visibly relaxed and then she smiled at Arlene. "How nice to see you, dear! Frank has been showing me pictures of the baby. My goodness, he is growing like a weed, isn't he?"

Arlene nodded.

Ruth went on quickly. "We're shopping for nursery furniture. We can use some of the old stuff from the attic, but we have to get new cribs for sure." She picked up a layette that was decorated with the movie mouse characters as babies. "This is sweet, isn't it?" she asked of the other two women. "This would work nicely for boys or girls. Or even a mixed pair!"

Arlene looked from the print to Laena. "You don't know yet?"

Laena shook her head. "Michael couldn't tell for sure on the ultrasound. He mentioned something about doing an amniocentesis, but wants to wait a bit longer. There is a specialist he'd want to do that procedure."

Arlene turned back to the different layette designs. "I used the Noah's Ark pattern. My mother suggested it, saying it would work for either."

Laena smiled. "You didn't know the sex either, before he was born then?"

Arlene shook her head. "Jeff wanted to try the ultrasound again, but I told him no. I wanted to keep it a surprise, just like they used to do."

Laena looked at the other woman for a long moment. Suddenly, for the first time, she saw her as a person, and not as the woman who had taken away her husband. She felt no resentment or rancor. In fact, she acknowledged that if Arlene had not come along, she would not have been living with Ruth and met Jack. She smiled after a moment. "That is how I feel. It's nice to have some mystery in these days when we know so much about everything."

Arlene met Laena's gaze and nodded. "So long as everything is going well and the baby is healthy—"

Ruth laughed, drawing the attention of the two younger women. "But you know how men are? They have to know everything there is to know. I caught Jack the other morning with a book on twin pregnancy. And I swear he flushed when he saw me standing there."

Laena was surprised. She hadn't seen Jack reading any books. She assumed he knew it all, having been through it before. Just then, a sales clerk approached and asked if she could help them find anything. Ruth said yes, and a few moments later they parted company with Arlene and continued their shopping expedition.

* * * * *

Jack walked in the front door later that afternoon and almost stumbled over all of the sacks and boxes scattered around. He chuckled to himself, and wondered how much of a dent in his bank account his two ladies had managed to make. He called out, "Hey! Anybody come home with all these purchases?"

Ruth came out of the kitchen. She was dressed to the nines in spite of the apron she wore. "Hush! I'm going out to dinner with Frank in a few minutes, but I've got dinner in the oven for you two for later. I sent Laena upstairs to nap for a bit. Why don't you go on up and I'll see you both later. I'll finish in the kitchen so I'll be ready for Frank."

Jack watched his mother disappear back into the kitchen. He set down his briefcase and made his way up the stairs. He entered the bedroom and found Laena was sprawled across the top of the covers, wearing only the sexy maternity bra and panties that he had splurged on for her. He stripped off his own clothes, down to his shorts and lay down behind her on the bed. He wrapped his arm across her and settled his head on the pillow beside hers. Listening to her quiet breathing, and letting the warmth of her body seep into him, he soon fell asleep as well.

Laena awoke slowly, feeling warm and cozy. A few moments passed before she realized that she wasn't alone in the bed. She glanced down and saw Jack's arm casually draped across her body, where her waist used to be. His hand lay flat over her rounded tummy. Without moving too much, she managed to undo the clasp at the front of her bra. Her heavy breasts quickly spread the cups and she took a deep breath.

A scant second later, almost as she took a deep breath of relief, Jack's hand slid up and under the topmost cup. His hand easily molded and massaged her breast. He slid closer.

She could feel his hard arousal pressing against her rounded cheeks.

Jack lightly kissed her shoulder. "How did the shopping go? I almost tripped over some of it when I got home."

Laena couldn't resist wiggling her bottom against his manhood. Jack's groan told of the effectiveness of her simple action. She slid her hand over his. "We ran into Arlene."

"Hell!"

Laena felt the tension in Jack at her announcement. She rubbed his hand lightly. "It's all right. Nothing happened, and we actually chatted for a few minutes like real grownups."

Jack chuckled at her attempt at humor. "Should I believe the meeting was that non-noxious? Nothing got broken, then?"

Laena laughed in response. "No, but I should warn you that your mother decided we wouldn't be using any of the old furniture after all."

Jack sighed deeply. "I'm not surprised. She has always been a big spender when it came to grandchildren. Did you decide which room you want to use?"

Laena's hand stopped rubbing Jack's. "I would like to use the small one here, if you don't mind."

"Hmm, since we sleep in here most nights, I'd considered making that an office. But if you want it for the nursery, we can do that. Maybe plan on moving the bedroom to my old room in a year or so?"

"Of course, we'd have to get started on it pretty quickly. So, we could move all of your things in here."

There was a pause, and then Jack replied. "Yes, that way we will both be here if they should decide to cry at the same time."

"Will we draw straws each time or take turns?"

Jack scooted closer, nuzzling her neck. He slid his hand down over her tummy and between her thighs. He groaned as the wetness between her soft lips coated his hand. He quickly pulled her panties down and off.

Laena rolled onto her back and looked up at Jack. He looked so handsome with a lock of hair falling down across his forehead. Reaching up, she gently pushed the errant lock back with her fingers. She smiled when she met his gaze.

Jack stopped. "Marry me, Laena."

Laena gasped in surprise. She had not expected a proposal of marriage. "Is this just for the good of the babies? You want to make everything legitimate, or whatever to satisfy gossip mongers?"

Jack shrugged. "I guess I'm an old-fashioned man after all. If it were just you and I then I would do whatever you wanted. It wouldn't matter to me. But we live in a society that still does care. This isn't the example I want to set for my sons, even at their age. And as far as Mother is concerned, I doubt she would ever say anything, one way or another."

"So?"

Jack smiled. He slid his hand to cup and began caressing the side of her face. "So, I want to stake a claim on you and the babies. I want it all legal and binding."

"I've got one failed marriage behind me already, Jack." Laena felt bound to point that fact out once more. She had assumed she would never marry again, yet hearing him ask her so casually to marry him, there had to be catch. Nothing in life was ever this easy or straightforward, that's what she'd thought. Nothing gone quite the way she had anticipated, especially since she'd met Jack. "There would be even more hurt—" her voice cracked from trying to hold back her tears, which struggled between joyful and fearful.

"That one doesn't count, honey. There is only you and I, and the future from now on. If you would prefer moving to another house or even another town so you won't have to run into Jeff or Arlene ever again, we can do that. Just tell me what you want, and I'll do my damnedest to make it happen." Jack lightly caressed her lower lip with his thumb.

Sniffling loudly, she shook her head. "No more running away for me. I won't let Jeff chase me off." She paused, knowing she needed to tell Jack something else she'd learned today. "Arlene found me alone again one more time before we left the store."

Jack stiffened. "What did she say?"

"I found out that Jeff is even more of a schmuck than I thought. Arlene told me she was so surprised to see I was pregnant because Jeff had told her I couldn't give him a child. He deliberately told her I was infertile." She stopped, still feeling herself reeling under the weight of his deception.

"What the he—" Jack cut off his expletive. He took a deep breath before he asked her, "Was that all she said?"

"Ruth was coming back and she was on major defensive mode." Laena smiled, remembering how protective the older woman had been.

"Yeah. She can be pretty fierce when somebody attacks her baby chick."

"Well, I'm not really her baby chick," Laena felt like she had to point it out.

"She already loves you like you are one of her daughters. I could tell she felt like that long before anyone knew you were pregnant. I admit that I couldn't see it at first until an old friend of mine pointed out the obvious." Jack shrugged. "He pointed out that you being here, available to live in the house, allowed my mother something more important than her well-meaning children. With you, Laena, Mother had her independence and the peace and comfort of remaining in the home she'd had for almost fifty years."

"Ruth gave me something as well, Jack." She paused as he grinned. Reaching out she touched the tip of his nose with her finger. "Besides you, I mean. She gave the sanctuary I needed to heal and recover. We traded."

"I need to say one thing and then we'll drop the subject, unless you bring it up." Jack reached out and ran his hand up and down her arm. "Any idea why Jeff would say that?"

"Jeff wanted to have an affair with Arlene, and she was holding out because he was married. This way he proved he was a victim… deprived of fatherhood? It's strange, Jack, but even as she started telling me, I had no doubt it was the truth."

"All right, we can check both of them off the list as reasons not to marry." Jack made an imaginary check mark in the air. "Do you want a different house to live in? I know the town isn't big, but would you prefer living in town?"

Laena chuckled. "Hmm, maybe I should be writing this down so I can remind you of all these offers in a year or two."

Jack shook his head. "You don't have to write it down, honey. I'll never forget it. So, are you willing to give me a chance?"

Laena nodded, the tears catching in her throat. The dam broke on her feelings. She couldn't keep them inside another second. Even if he didn't echo them back, his actions told her that he cared. She knew she was standing at the precipice and it was time to take the leap of faith… a risk. "I love you, Jack." Her voice cracked and she sniffled quickly before she went on. "I swore I wouldn't fall in love again, but somehow you got into my heart."

"I love you, too, Laena. Our start may have been out of the ordinary, but from now on, nothing matters but you, our family and me. Marry me?"

She started to say "yes" but stopped as she remembered something. "What about David and Daniel? They may like me as the woman who lived with their grandmother, but as a stepmother, it is quite possible they will protest, and say 'no way!'"

"You are off base, sweetheart. Both boys have gone out of their way, although I'm sure they discussed it beforehand, to come into the office and tell me how happy they are about you and me, and the babies. They are very excited to be older siblings." Jack paused for a moment. "I was very proud of each one, at how composed they were. David seems to have matured since he began working part-time on the farm and still takes a few classes here and there towards his degree."

Laena knew she was being silly, but she felt the need to know, for sure. "Do you ever wonder how things might have been, Jack, if only Celia had not died?"

Jack shook his head. "I might have, in the early years, but I'm not a man to worry over the past, or things that can never be. Since I've met you, Laena, you are the only woman I think about. Celia was my past, and I loved her then. You are my future, and I love you now. I want to be with you and our babies, and the boys. I know I'm older than you, and I know there is a chance I won't be here to see the twins graduate from college."

Laena couldn't stop the gasp or the tears that welled up in her eyes. "No! You are in excellent shape."

"Hush, my love. I'm only saying what could be, and that I will have preparations made so that if something should happen, you and the babies will be protected and taken care of."

"Thank you, Jack, but all I want is you."

"I know, darling, and after this is said, we won't dwell on it. We will live our lives one day, and one moment, at a time, so we can savor each and every minute we have.

We're going to have a beautiful life together." He lightly rubbed his thumb over one cheek, brushing off the tear there. "Marry me?"

"Yes, Jack, I'll marry you. I'm not perfect but I'll do my best. I'm not that much of a cook."

"Mother enjoys cooking, and I like to do it as well. When Mom can't any longer, I'll hire a housekeeper. I want you to keep up with your pottery," Jack added.

"I think you are the too-perfect one. I love you, Jack."

"Just keep thinking those thoughts, honey! I'll remind you of it on our fifth wedding anniversary!"

She lifted her face to meet Jack's gentle kiss, which was the first of countless thousands to come in the years ahead. After a moment, she pulled back. "Why our *fifth* anniversary?"

"I can just imagine how chaotic our lives will be with two kindergarteners!"

"What is this? Despair from the man who managed the White House for eight years?"

Jack growled as he covered her mouth for his kiss. "Let me show you some of my hands-on management techniques."

Laena discovered just how thorough and detailed Jack could be.

Chapter Eighteen

Jack sipped his beer slowly, not wanting to have too much on this Christmas Eve. A quick glance at the clock over the bar told him they had at least another hour before being allowed back in the house.

Two hours earlier, he'd been happily preparing for the onslaught of family for a tree-trimming party. To his and Laena's surprise, his brothers and brothers-in-law arrived and practically kidnapped him and brought him here, to the small local bar near the edge of town.

His mother had reassured that all was well. The tree would still get trimmed and Laena would be fine.

Here he sat, starting his third hour of drinking moderately while his family engaged in various games of chance. He couldn't say for sure, but he'd bet he was the soberest one of the bunch right about now. Good thing they had all come in Michael's new full-sized sports utility vehicle. And it looked like he would be driving them home.

He was pretty sure he'd been hijacked, and the other men sent away, so the women could have full use of the house for a baby shower. The kids were probably decorating while the ladies had punch, cake and opened all the presents. It bummed him out a little because he would have enjoyed watching as Laena opened the gifts. Each one revealing something interesting, cute and either useful or useless.

Instead, he was here…sharing what Michael had termed "brother bonding brunch".

He had asked where the food was for the brunch part of it.

Tom, Janet's husband and ever the wisecracker, held up the bowls of peanuts and pretzels. "Gourmet, too!"

"Well, fellas, is it going to be another round?" the pretty brunette waitress asked them politely.

"What do you think, guys? One more?" Hank asked, emptying his glass.

Ring!

Brrring…brrrring!

"Let's get it on…"

Tingle ling. Tingle ling.

"When Irish eyes are smiling…"

Jack watched as all five of his tablemates reached for their cell phones. That's when he realized that his was still on the charger.

* * * * *

Laena shifted on the sofa, trying to ease the ache in her lower back. Tiredness seemed to be a never-ending part of life lately, as did sleepless nights. Christmas was tomorrow, so hopefully the babies would come soon after that.

"Over here, David!" Daniel called out, catching her attention.

Turning her head, Laena watched as David tossed one of Ruth's ornaments like a football. Ruth would cringe if she saw them doing that.

"Hey, you two! Stop that!" Janet was already sailing in full tilt across the room in their direction. "Those are heirlooms, even if they are a little time-worn."

Daniel held up the abused ornament.

Even from her seat across the room, Laena could see the chips of missing shiny paint.

"Look at this!" Daniel turned the ornament around, revealing a large hole on the other side.

"Stop impugning my Christmas decorations, Daniel," Ruth admonished her grandson as she entered the front living room. "Now, where were we?" she added, walking over and sitting across from Laena.

"It's time for Aunt Laena to open my present!" All eyes turned to where Kristi stood next to the bowl of candy put out for the baby shower. One hand held an envelope, and the other was in the candy.

"It's from both of us, Auntie Laena," Karen added, sticking her tongue out at her sister, even as she pushed her hand into the candy.

"How can she open it from over there, nits?" Fifteen-year-old Melissa admonished her cousins, grabbing the colorful envelope, and walking it over to Laena. "It's also from me and Mandy."

"Hey!" Daniel cried out his protest. "You guys went foursies on a gift. Grams said the most we could do was two of us."

Melissa huffed at her older cousin, tossed her long dark hair over her shoulder and sat back down on the floor at the coffee table, a few feet in front of Laena. "We aren't cheap. You'll see when you open it."

Laena turned over the bright yellow and pink envelope, carefully opening it. The twins, Karen and

Kristi, had obviously assisted in the making of the card and decorating the outside. "I'm sure it will be wonderful," she said, smiling at Melissa and then at two girls still at the candy bowl.

Melissa called out, "Mandy! Get in here! Laena's opening our present!"

Laena pulled out the card, looked at the decorated front of the card then opened it. A small booklet fell out, bounced off her rounded belly and hit the floor. "Sorry," she mumbled.

"I'll get it," Melissa assured her. "Go ahead and read it."

"Aloud!" Karen and Kristi yelled from their position.

"Okay. 'To our newest ant.'" She looked twice and saw a small "u" was written in just above the "n." She smiled and nodded, accepting the other booklet from Melissa. "Let me see, oh yes. 'Use these whenever you need time with Uncle Jack.'"

Janet glanced at the girls by the candy dish and added softly, "Or when you need time away from the kids!"

Laena opened the booklet. "Oh, babysitting coupons! How thoughtful of you girls! Thank you all!"

"Each one is good for one session, not like just for an hour," Melissa pointed out, leaning across the coffee table, indicating the writing on the first coupon. "Mandy and I will both come each time, unless someone—" she paused to turn and look at her one year older cousin, "—has a date with a certain high-school quarterback."

"Hey, snitch!" Mandy called out from the doorway, where she was leaning against the jamb.

Sally grinned. "I knew already, daughter dearest. It was a little hard to miss the way he tripped when he ran past you during the beginning cheer last Friday."

Mandy's cheeks flushed, and she spoke quickly. "If Melissa is busy, then I will bring Karen and Kristi with me to help baby sit."

"And vice versa," Melissa added quickly.

"This is so sweet," Laena could feel her tears rushing up once more. "There must be at least ten coupons in here!"

"Twenty!" Four young female voices added at the same time.

Laena's tears turned to laughter. "Do I get a hug as well?" she asked a moment later.

"Of course!" Melissa leaned over the table and Laena leaned forward, rising up a little. The twins rushed forward, and she had to come a bit further —

"You squeezed her too hard, Karen!" Kristi accused her sister a second later.

"Did not!" Karen protested quickly.

Kristi snapped back. "Did too! You made her pee!"

Laena would not have chosen that way to tell everyone her water had just broken, but it got the job done in a concise way.

Calamitous was too mild to cover what happened after that.

"Oh, Ruth, I'm so sorry about the rug!" Laena said the first thing that popped into her head.

"I don't give two hoots about the rug," Ruth reassured her.

Cindy clapped her hands to get everyone's attention. "Organization is the key here!"

Jean, Patrick's wife, was already shooing people out of her way to reach Laena's side. "Are you having labor pains?"

Laena straightened slowly. "My back has hurt quite a bit today… I thought it was just — "

Sally, a former obstetrical nurse, turned from telling her boys to stay out of the candy. "Are they spaced? How far apart are they?"

"I'm not sure. I kept telling myself to ignore it, especially once the party started." Laena explained.

Ruth, who was still seated on the sofa, spoke up. "Her bag is in the front hall closet."

"Thank you, Mother," Janet replied then turned to yell across the room. "David! Daniel! One of you bring the car round front of the house, while the other grabs her suitcase from the hall closet."

Laena looked over in time to see the two young men totally caught off-guard as they realized she was having the baby, now!

With good intentions, they both ran full speed forward and into one another. They bounced into the tree and down came the half-decorated, tinsel-strewn, nine-foot tree.

Fifteen minutes later, the bright red sports car pulled to a jerking stop outside the emergency room. A discussion had convinced everyone that Laena couldn't climb the distance to the van or the sport utility vehicle, so the jaunty little car was chosen.

Laena refused to get in until a large plastic bag was put over the seat and floor. They were the first car in the tinsel-strewn caravan that started to the hospital.

While the boys, David and Daniel, climbed up and out of the tree, Ruth had crossed to the phone, using the automatic dial feature to ring Jack's cellular phone. Two seconds later, they all turned as the phone in its charger on the hallway table screamed its presence. En masse, Laena's five sisters-in-law pulled out their own phones and dialed.

* * * * *

The first car Jack saw as he pulled into the emergency parking lot was his mother's sports car, with the top down. Parking beside it, he saw plastic bags on the passenger seat and tinsel everywhere. Gathering his "bonded" family, he steered them to the top floor, where the obstetrical unit was located.

The waiting room was overflowing with Spencer family members. It didn't look at first glance as if anyone had been left behind. He located his mother and went to her first. "Where's Laena?"

"She's been taken back and they admitted her."

Hank came up, leaning slightly on his wife, Cindy. "So, it isn't false labor?"

"No, dear. Not everyone thinks a burp is labor pain." Cindy told her husband in a short tone. "I think you should sit down."

"I'm not drunk, Cynthia, and I never saw a woman burp as much as you did with our first." Hank protested as his wife turned and steered him to a chair.

"Who do I see, or where do I go?" Jack asked his mother.

Ruth turned, her gaze scanning the room. "Sally will know, dear. Sally, can you help Jack?"

"Of course, I can. Michael waved and headed back already. Laena's obstetrician is already here as well. Come with me, Jack."

Nodding, Jack started to follow Sally. He looked back over the sea of faces in the waiting room. How different this was from the first time he was here. Only his mother and father had been here because Celia's parents were out of state on vacation. They had tried to make arrangements to get back, but the babies arrived before they did.

Jack smiled. Everything was different. He was a little sad that Celia missed seeing their sons grow up, but he knew she watched over them from above. Now, his family was quite large and happy.

Dear God, please bring Laena and our babies through this safely, he prayed silently.

Yes. God willing, his family would increase by two before tomorrow dawned!

Epilogue

The hospital waiting room was a madhouse the night Laena went into labor. She surprised them all by carrying the babies for a little over eight months. But once she got started, she tried to tell Michael that he should change his bet on the time of the first birth.

Michael shook his head, muttering about first babies and women and mothers.

Laena and the nurses had looked at one another and just shrugged.

Of course, when Michael had to come running back upstairs ten minutes later, they all laughed and got to say "I told you so" at least once. Jack held her hand throughout her labor, huffing and puffing right along with her. And he enjoyed seeing his brother proved wrong, in spite of the added stress on him. Her obstetrician let him cut the umbilical cord. Sally finally set her husband in the corner and told him he wasn't the doctor of record and to sit down!

Daniel won the pool with 11:59 p.m. for twin A, and by the time the sibling arrived, he eagerly told everyone that not only did he win the money, but he also got to name the babies. For all of their lives, Keeley and Kelsey Spencer heard how their big brother almost got to call them Fog and Leg! This of course, he pointed out with great glee and relish, was short for Foghorn and Leghorn.

Needless to say, the girls got into a lot of spats with their older brothers, but they all did indeed, live pretty much happily ever after.

The End

Enjoy this excerpt from
Cattleman
© Copyright Mlyn Hurn 2004

Jim made no effort to curb the smile curving his lips upward. Seeing Julie Bradley, half-undressed, wet and alone, was making this feel like his birthday rather than hers. She was his present! Immediately he realized that three years had not made the least difference in how he felt about her. But when she was eighteen and her father sent her east, he was just starting out with his own ranching concern separate from his father's and had nothing to offer a woman. Or more precisely, he had little resources to comprise a respectable dowry should Jason Bradley have demanded one.

And there was the fact that whenever he and Julie were together sparks usually flew in all directions. But ever since she was sixteen, there had been this sort of magical transformation in her, or perhaps it had only been within himself. After that, every time he saw Julie, he knew that it was desire that had prompted him to antagonize her. Basically he did anything, good or bad, just like a kid, to get her attention. Often it was bad, yet there were times when her eyes would meet his that he knew she felt something, and it had nothing to do with dislike.

"You should have told me you wanted this to be a swimming party," he murmured softly. He knew damn well her being in the water had little to do with a desire to swim in it. But to be honest, seeing her wearing the cut down version of long-john underwear, the way it clung to her curvaceous body like a second skin, was more than a little strain on his nervous system. Right now his own body was pressing him for some relief.

Logically he could do two things: he could ride away or he could dismount and see what would happen. Almost before he realized it, his body was already in motion. Julie spoke immediately, but the words fell on his suddenly deaf ears.

"Oh no, Jim, your boots will be ruined!"

Jim shook his head and reached down to grasp her hand. She accepted it and as he pulled her up, the blood dripping from her other hand caught his attention. "Holy cow, Julie, what the hell happened to your hand?"

"I caught it on a splinter of wood on that bench. Technically that makes it your fault, right?"

Jim looked up from his inspection of her hand to meet her eyes. What he saw, though, didn't seem to match what she'd just spoken. Dropping her hand, he took a step toward her.

Julie froze. Her stomach was doing flip-flops and she was sure Jim was going to kiss her. Every fiber of her being was shouting "yes" and she took a step closer. She could feel her heart pounding harder in her chest than it ever had before. Desperately she wanted to feel his lips on hers. Many times she had dreamed of this happening. Now, less than a foot separated them.

Black Devil, the stallion Jim had ridden into the water, nickered and began walking toward the grass-covered bank. It was just enough to break the spell and they both pulled back. Julie felt her cheeks flame hotly with embarrassment. She had realized that if Jim had wanted to kiss her, the horse couldn't have distracted him. Obviously, in her mind, she was alone in her feelings. Quickly she stumbled back to the bank and then onto the bench. Looking around, it took her a few moments to locate her discarded shirt.

Jim grabbed the shirt before she had the chance and then he sat down beside her. "What were you planning on doing?" he asked with a smile.

Julie looked over at him and saw that he had also picked up the discarded bottle. It surprised her to realize that she had drunk enough of it so that it showed barely half-full. Deciding to ignore the subject of the bottle, she answered him as she reached for the shirt he was still holding. "I am tearing a piece of my shirt to wrap around my hand. Then everything will be fine."

Jim, though, apparently didn't agree as he continued to hold the shirt, shifting it just beyond her reach. "Speaking for myself, I wouldn't object. You've always been a woman to dress for yourself, Julie, but in that wet shirt…"

Julie saw that Jim was looking at her chest. Slowly she bent her neck and looked down. It took a moment for her to realize that she looked just like she did when she was sitting naked in the tub. The thin material disguised nothing from any onlooker. And Jim was most definitely looking.

"Julie?"

Looking up, she saw the intent look on Jim's face and the fire in his eyes. Normally she'd say he was angry with her, but suddenly she knew it wasn't his usual fury or disapproval. No. What she was seeing was the same as she'd seen on the faces of the young men she'd met in Boston. They had all had a hard time understanding that she wasn't interested in them. But she liked the look in his eyes. All they needed—

"Hey! So this is where the birthday girl has been hiding!"

Startled, she and Jim both turned and saw his brother, Tony, walking toward them. A second later she felt her shirt being draped across the front of her.

"Julie accidentally cut her hand," Jim spoke as he tossed the bottle into the bushes next to the bench. Turning to Julie, he said, "I'll have you put on my shirt, and then we can tear a strip off yours."

"You need any help?" Tony asked and started to walk toward the bench.

Jim stood up and walked to meet his brother. "No, but if you wouldn't mind taking Devil with you, I'd appreciate it."

Julie watched the two men, craning her neck to see. She saw Tony nodding several times before he turned, grabbed Black Devil's dangling reins and walked back out of the secluded area. Quickly, as Jim started back toward her, she pulled her shirt on. When he reached the bench, she had managed just two buttons, but at least she was covered. The thought of remaining exposed in front of him had been too taxing to contemplate. There was also the mental picture dancing around in her head of Jim minus his shirt, and it had her heart racing and her breathing becoming more labored.

"You can go too, Jim, if you'd like. I'll just stay here for a bit and put some pressure on this. It will be fine in a few minutes, I'm sure."

Julie wasn't all that surprised when she heard fabric tearing. Looking up, she saw that he had torn the lower edge, about three inches wide, from his shirt. Disappointment flooded through her as she realized that he'd done it while still wearing his shirt, only pulling it free from his jeans. Without saying another word, he picked her hand up and deftly bound the shirt around it. Her emotions were becoming more jumbled and confusing with each passing second. She was sad he was ending this interlude so succinctly, yet confused because she should have been glad…right?

"Thank you," she murmured when he released the small, neat knot he had tied.

"No problem, but you should come to the house so I can put a clean dressing on it."

Julie hated the awkward feelings overwhelming her at the moment. "Maybe a little bit later, so no one sees us going in together."

Jim turned away abruptly, buttoning what was left of his shirt as he did so. "Yeah, it's important to keep that never ending feud going between us. Enjoy your party."

About the author:

Mlyn lives in Indiana, USA. She worked as a Registered Nurse for 23 years in Pediatrics. Reading Barbara Cartland and Harlequin romance novels in high school spurred her to start writing. She did technical writing for her employers until she started writing erotica four years ago. She began her own website for people to view her stories. Mlyn is single and lives with her cranky cat Georgia, whom she named after her favorite artist for inspiration, Georgia O'Keeffe.

Mlyn welcomes mail from readers. You can write to her c/o Ellora's Cave Publishing at 1056 Home Avenue, Akron OH 44310-3502.

Why an electronic book?

We live in the Information Age—an exciting time in the history of human civilization in which technology rules supreme and continues to progress in leaps and bounds every minute of every hour of every day. For a multitude of reasons, more and more avid literary fans are opting to purchase e-books instead of paperbacks. The question to those not yet initiated to the world of electronic reading is simply: *why?*

1. *Price*. An electronic title at Ellora's Cave Publishing and Cerridwen Press runs anywhere from 40-75% less than the cover price of the <u>exact same title</u> in paperback format. Why? Cold mathematics. It is less expensive to publish an e-book than it is to publish a paperback, so the savings are passed along to the consumer.

2. *Space*. Running out of room to house your paperback books? That is one worry you will never have with electronic novels. For a low one-time cost, you can purchase a handheld computer designed specifically for e-reading purposes. Many e-readers are larger than the average handheld, giving you plenty of screen room. Better yet, hundreds of titles can be stored within your new library—a single microchip. (Please note that Ellora's Cave and Cerridwen Press does not endorse any specific brands. You can check our website at www.ellorascave.com o

www.cerridwenpress.com for customer recommendations we make available to new consumers.)

3. *Mobility.* Because your new library now consists of only a microchip, your entire cache of books can be taken with you wherever you go.

4. *Personal preferences are accounted for.* Are the words you are currently reading too small? Too large? Too...**ANNOYING**? Paperback books cannot be modified according to personal preferences, but e-books can.

5. *Instant gratification.* Is it the middle of the night and all the bookstores are closed? Are you tired of waiting days—sometimes weeks—for online and offline bookstores to ship the novels you bought? Ellora's Cave Publishing sells instantaneous downloads 24 hours a day, 7 days a week, 365 days a year. Our e-book delivery system is 100% automated, meaning your order is filled as soon as you pay for it.

Those are a few of the top reasons why electronic novels are displacing paperbacks for many an avid reader. As always, Ellora's Cave and Cerridwen Press welcomes your questions and comments. We invite you to email us at service@ellorascave.com, service@cerridwenpress.com or write to us directly at: 1056 Home Ave. Akron OH 44310-3502.